There was Rob Kilgerrin!

He stood near a Grecian-style pillar, his familiar grin riding his lips as he watched the dancers spinning round and round in the glistening ballroom.

Alicia's heart leaped up—and she did also, interrupting her aunt's autobiographical monologue with "I see a friend . . ."

Her aunt's eyebrows met in a frown. "Are you going to gallop right up to that young man? That's brazen. You must allow *him* to approach."

Impatiently Alicia explained. "Normally I should do so, of course, but as I have almost made up my mind to marry Mr. Kilgerrin, I—"

"Marry him! Don't be absurd, child. Your uncle and I will decide that. And why hasn't he spoken to Tobias?"

"Mr. Kilgerrin has not yet proposed marriage to me," Alicia replied. "Do lower your voice, Aunt. I want this all to be a surprise to him. Men in general prefer to think that *they* have initiated these matters. But you really must excuse me. I think Miss Smedley is headed in his direction, and she is looking particularly well tonight, so it is urgent that I speak to him before she does."

AGENT
OF
LOVE

by
Jillian Kearny

WARNER BOOKS

A Warner Communications Company

Chapter 1

It was always the same.

Mounted on the great ebony stallion, galloping along the shadow-striped lane between the enormous twisted oaks. Her long auburn hair whipping out behind, lashing at the midnight air, Alicia Kingsley clutched at the reins and urged the horse onward.

Something was pursuing her, was pulling closer. She could hear the heavy hooves pounding up the dust of the lane. She never looked back, though. She had to get away from there, as far from Ravenshaw Court as she could. And she must never return.

Head bent low, the girl kept her eyes straight ahead. Clouds scudded across the moon, making the light thin. The forest leaves clattered in the dark wind.

Alicia knew what was coming, but somehow

could not avoid it. A chasm loomed suddenly ahead, cutting jaggedly across the roadway.

She jerked at the reins, leather slicing at her palms, but the horse would not stop. It went sailing over the chasm, powerful legs churning at the air.

They never reached the other side.

Instead, the stallion snorting wildly, they fell. Down and down into the chasm, until all the pale milky moonlight was gone, until thick blackness filled in.

Falling and falling, rushing toward the other bodies far below. Bodies long dead, bones broken and shattered by the long drop down through darkness.

Then Alicia felt something smooth and solid beneath her hand. The darkness diminished, and the barefooted girl saw one thin wedge of moonlight coming down from the leaded skylight.

She held on tighter to the balustrade of the great twisting staircase. "I was running away from Ravenshaw again," she said, almost aloud. "I never succeed."

Alicia glanced around. She'd wandered farther tonight, come down nearly to the foyer of her uncle's London house. Always the same dream.

In the nightmare she was always pursued, chased again and again through the shadowy midnight countryside around Ravenshaw Court. She'd grown up in that great sprawling house, been very happy there. Happy until—

"Dante, you are a naughty creature!"

Something had come yapping down the staircase, was now growling at Alicia's heels.

From above again came the dry raspy voice. "Dante, leave poor dear Alicia alone. Do you hear me, you little blackguard?"

Bending, Alicia caught the snarling little lap-dog up by his gem-encrusted collar. "It's all right, Queen Bess. Poor old Dante has very few teeth left, and none of those very formidable."

"Don't go dangling him in that manner, child. He'll choke."

Alicia let the buff-colored old dog drop to the runner. "We mustn't permit that."

Yowling, Dante went scrambling back up to his mistress.

Queen Bess stood on the landing, one gnarled hand gripping the newel post and the other holding aloft a sputtering candle. "Have you had another of your seizures, Alicia?" she inquired in her ancient brittle voice.

The girl looked up at the old woman. The candle light did not flatter Elizabeth Copplestone, whom all were required to call Queen Bess. Someone had once coined the nickname with affection, long ago, in the early years of the reign of George III.

Queen Bess wore a faded paisley shawl over her narrow shoulders and a lace-ridden cap atop her head. The thick white powder she applied to her raddled and wrinkled face was much in evidence. The dead-white powder coupled with her long white nightgown gave her a decidedly ghostly appearance. "Stop that at once, Dante!"

The venerable little animal was attempting to hide in the folds of the nightdress, taking up a position between her stick-thin ankles.

"It was only a bad dream," explained Alicia as she carefully climbed the stairs toward her great-aunt. "Nothing to worry over, really."

"Nothing to worry over indeed!" The old woman produced one of her incredulous laughs. "You

7

go running through the house at an ungodly hour, screaming the name of that miserable country house which you are well quit of and—"

"I wasn't aware I'd cried out, Queen Bess."

"Child, you always cry out," the old woman assured her. "If I needed any further proof Tanner had been tippling the port from our cellar, his failure to be awakened by your caterwauling certainly provides it. Since Meggs is as deaf as a post, she's been able to sleep through these increasingly frequent attacks of yours as well. Otherwise I am sure we'd be the talk of Darkside Square, if not of all London."

"Young women often have bad dreams." Alicia had reached the landing, stood facing her aunt.

"I well remember Major Malley's last years, poor man. He took to careening through that lovely house of his in Surrey, waving the selfsame sword he'd used so nobly against various heathen enemies of England. Waving the sword and crying out for vengeance against someone named Lovesey. They never learned who Lovesey might have been, and the poor major was locked away without ever revealing the identity. It has always, however, been my opinion that Lovesey was the exact same fellow with whom the major's very much younger—"

"Aunt Elizabeth, I'm sure I'll soon outgrow these . . . little nocturnal excursions," said the girl. "I'm truly sorry I've been upsetting you."

"You upset poor little Dante as well." The dancing candle flame produced new and changing wrinkles on her white face. "He's an extremely old animal, Alicia, and I fear his noble heart is not in the best of shape."

"Too much rich food," suggested the girl, "and far from enough exercise."

8

"Exercise? If he keeps hopping off my counterpane each night and chasing after you, child, he'll soon have as much exercise as your uncle's foxhounds."

Smiling the quiet smile which did so much to intrigue the young men of her acquaintance, Alicia reached out to touch her great-aunt's leathery wrist. "Let's return to bed now," she said. "I'm truly sorry about all the trouble I'm causing the household."

"We really must get to the root of this problem, child. The past month you've had far too many of these fits. Far too many." The old woman's eyes narrowed. "I'm wondering, Alicia, if another consultation with Dr. Marryat isn't in order."

Alicia all at once found it difficult to breathe. She shivered once, hugging herself. "I," she managed to say, "hardly think such a course is necessary. Aside from these bad dreams, I am quite disgustingly healthy."

"Perhaps," continued her gaunt great-aunt, "you're in no condition to attend Lady Westlake's ball this Friday evening. It might be wise to send our regrets and—"

"We'll attend," Alicia told her. She had reasons, one particular reason, rather, for wishing very much to be at the function. "So far, you know, I have never behaved in any unusual way in public."

"No, when in the public eye you are a most fetching young creature," conceded Queen Bess. "Although, there are those who imply you are a bit too outspoken and modish."

"In the long run, Aunt, such a reputation doesn't harm one." Alicia stepped back, turned toward the corridor which led to her bedchamber. "We'll consider the question of the ball settled."

"Very well," said the old woman. "I do, however, feel this problem of yours is more serious than you pretend, Alicia."

"Nonsense." Alicia smiled, walking away along the shadowed corridor. When she was no longer facing her great-aunt, the smile dropped away from her pretty face.

Chapter 2

Dr. Noah Marryat slowly brought one stained hand up toward his purplish nose. He thrust a pinch of glistening powder into his left nostril. His large head tilted back, and he gave forth three satisfied sneezes. "Ah," he said in his rumbling voice.

"I have always considered the taking of snuff," said Queen Bess, "a most disgusting habit."

"And I, madam, have long thought that butter-colored cur with which you decorate your lap a most disgusting piece of gammon," returned the short-statured doctor as he brushed at his snuff-spattered cravat. "You did not, I am more than certain, arrange this hurried interview with me merely to discuss our mutual loathing for each other."

"Far from it. That would require too much of the day and I must prepare for Lady Westlake's ball on the morrow." The old woman studied the doctor, absently knuckling the wrinkled head of the dozing Dante.

Dr. Marryat turned his back on the seated woman to gaze at the small feeble fire which crackled in his deep stone fireplace. "Your note indicated some urgency, madam."

"I am fairly certain," Queen Bess informed him, "something is happening to Alicia."

"Can you, please, be more specific?"

"The girl has been behaving in a most unusual manner, my dear doctor."

"Alicia is a very high-spirited girl."

"Of that I am well aware. What I allude to in the present instance, Dr. Marryat, is the series of somnambulistic attacks she has been suffering these past few weeks."

The little doctor turned slowly around. From his waistcoat pocket he extracted a monocle, which he inserted in his wrinkle-rimmed left eye. "Be so good as to provide me with some further details."

"The poor girl, to put it most simply, walks in her sleep." Queen Bess patted the snoring lapdog several times. "Roams the halls like a veritable apparition, doctor, and screams out the name of her birthplace."

Marryat's eyes widened, causing his monocle to pop free and dangle across the smeared front of his waistcoat. "Ravenshaw Court?"

"Precisely, in a most loud and carrying voice." The old woman nodded her turbaned head. "Were it not for the fact Tanner has most usually fallen into a drunken stupor by the hour Alicia suffers her nearly nightly—"

"She says nothing about . . ." Marryat scuttled

toward her across the carpet of his study. "About what she might have *seen* at Ravenshaw?"

"Thus far, no. Although I live in continual dread she may."

Shaking his head, the doctor said, "It is most unlikely, madam. Despite your feelings toward me, you must be aware of my genuine gifts. The great Dr. Franz Mesmer has no more successful a follower in all of England. Indeed, even on the Continent I—"

"Boasting won't help any of us, Marryat, should Alicia recollect what she witnessed that night."

"She will never remember," answered Dr. Marryat. "She cannot."

"Then what does this agitated behavior of hers indicate? If you ask me, she is struggling to recall what—"

"No one, to my knowledge, has solicited you for a medical opinion." He eased over to the articulated skeleton hanging from a copper stand in the darkest corner of his dark-paneled study. "There is no real danger, none at all. What the girl is undergoing is not uncommon in cases such as this. I have done my work well, exceedingly well. See to it, madam, you yourself do not betray us by flapping about town like a frightened jackdaw."

"You claim you did your work well," said Queen Bess, narrowed eyes watching the little man as he began to tap the glazed and grinning skull with stubby fingers. "Should it turn out you did not, then we will all of us come to—"

"Within a few months, a few short months at best, it shan't matter," promised Dr. Marryat. "If you and your dear nephew are seriously concerned, there is a quite simple solution. One which, if your addled brain can recall it, I offered to you both that night at Ravenshaw."

Queen Bess shook her old head vehemently. "Do you think either Tobias or I would ever allow any real harm to come to the child? She is, after all, the only daughter of Tobias's poor departed sister. It would be a cruel uncle indeed who—"

"These are cruel times, madam, and if we are to assist the cause we all believe in we must be prepared to resort to cruel measures."

The old woman rose up so swiftly the dreaming Dante tumbled off her lap and hit the floor with a thump. "I do not intend to listen any further to such outlandish suggestions."

"Then I respectfully bid you good morning," said Dr. Marryat.

"Good day, sir." Petticoats crackling, the old woman spun and, with the slightly dazed dog trotting in her wake, went storming out of the doctor's Berkeley Square residence.

Chapter 3

The bare fist came hurtling straight at his handsome chin.

Grinning, Rob Kilgerrin dodged and had the satisfaction of hearing the fist go whistling harmlessly by. "Not as swift as you might be," he told his opponent.

"It's me noddle, gov," explained the Brighton Butcher, bobbing and then feinting a left jab at Kilgerrin's upper torso. "Took somethin' of a bulldosin' in me recent encounter with the Holborn Hedgehog."

Parrying the hard right the Butcher attempted to land, Kilgerrin got in two telling punches to the bigger man's midsection. "You must learn," he advised, "not to advertise your blows quite so obviously."

"Most of the blokes I tangle with ain't got peepers quite so keen as yours."

"Possibly so." Kilgerrin was a lanky, well-muscled young man in his late twenties. Stripped to the waist now, his dark curling hair glistening, he maintained the slightly quirky grin on his face as he sparred with the Brighton Butcher.

The two men boxed silently, with the exception of an occasional pained grunt from the Butcher, for several minutes more. Warm stripes of afternoon sunlight cut across the high, white-walled gymnasium from the three slanting skylights.

"Ha, there's one for me!" The Butcher had delivered a smashing blow to Kilgerrin's ribs.

The young man went stumbling back across the roped-off, padded ring. "Serves me right," he acknowledged. "I was woolgathering."

"Got to keep your noddle on the game at hand, gov."

"Sound advice." Kilgerrin came charging at his head-shaved antagonist. He got under the larger man's guard, connected twice.

The Butcher woofed out breath, staggering.

Before Kilgerrin could close in on him, a high white door on his left popped open.

His man, Rumsford, entered the home gymnasium with a robe and a large towel over one plump arm. His stubby forefinger was stroking his broad flat nose.

Kilgerrin, brushing a forelock off his brow, stepped away from the heavy-breathing Butcher. "I'm afraid we'll have to conclude our lesson in pugilism for today."

"Blessed if I know who's teachin' who, gov." The big man rested a huge fist on the rope, sucking in breath through his open mouth. "Will you be attendin' me next match? We've a contest arranged with Beau Saintly, and I'm more than sure I can take the bloke this time."

"Pass me the word on the location of the bout, and I'll do my best to be there," promised Kilgerrin, swinging with ease out of the roped ring. "I take it we have a visitor, Rumsford?"

Rumsford handed his grinning young master the fluffy towel. "An intruder, rather, should you wish my candid opinion, sir," said the plump man in his piping voice. "He's fuming about in the drawing room, rearranging all my floral arrangements, pillaging books from off their shelves, and polluting the air with one of his malodorous cheroots."

"From that description my guest can only be Lord MacQuarrie," said Kilgerrin in a lowered voice as he toweled his bare chest and back.

"You are absolutely, unfortunately, correct, sir."

Passing the towel back, Kilgerrin slipped into the robe. "Urgent business?"

"So his lordship growled while laying waste to the furnishings."

Turning, the young man waved toward the ring. "Next week at the same time?"

"Right you are, gov. Unless Beau proves a good deal more ferocious than I expect."

Leaving the gymnasium, Kilgerrin strode along the shadowy hallway of his townhouse. Gray smoke was billowing out of the drawing room, along with sounds of agitated motion. "You have a definite knack, Lord Mac, for turning the most civilized surroundings into a bear pit," remarked the young man on entering.

Lord MacQuarrie was a tall, lean man of sixty-one. He was attired in a cocoa-brown frock coat and beige drill breeches; between his thin bloodless lips protruded a twisted and blackish cigar. "Haven't given up your interest in the Fancy, I see," he said, dropping the leatherbound book he'd been thumbing through onto the piano with a thunk. "Inviting all manner of ruffians into this pleasant and stately home. Why, your late father would—"

"It was my father who first introduced me to the pleasures of boxing, Lord Mac." With a grin, he seated himself on the piano bench. "Any gentleman worth his salt, according to my father, ought to be able to defend himself."

"Self-defence is one thing, Rob, while brawling with fellows who delight in such outlandish names as the Highgate Assassin and Ben Churl and the Brighton Butcher and Lord knows what other grating sobriquets is quite another business. Even if this pugilism weren't an illegal pastime, it should hardly be the occupation of a man of quality."

"I'm only an amateur," Kilgerrin reminded his visitor. Absently he commenced playing an Irish ballad on the piano, "And the estate, I find, gets on much better without my attentions. The manager tells me so, anyway." He began humming quietly in a pleasant tenor.

Lord MacQuarrie began circling the drawing room, trailing smoke like a Thames barge. "You take life much too lightly, Rob."

"It is too brief and fleeting to take at all seriously." He ceased playing, folded his hands, and watched the agitated older man. "Now then, Lord Mac, what exactly is the purpose of your visit? Judging from your state of vexation, this is more than a social call."

"Have I time for social chitchat with the world in such a sorry shape?" He shook his head, sending smoke wisping in two directions. "Bonaparte may be breathing down our necks at any moment, no man can afford to be calm."

One-handed, Kilgerrin played a snatch of a French air on the piano. "Is there further news in that direction?"

"Rumor and more rumor is all we have, Rob. Very little of substance, which is why I am here to urge you to procure more information for us."

"I begin to doubt I much fancy myself in the role of procurer," said young Kilgerrin. "You still suspect, then, that Alicia Kingsley is somehow involved in all this?"

"The girl is probably as innocent as a suckling babe," MacQuarrie responded. "Her uncle, however, is quite another bushel of potatoes, my boy. We are relatively certain meetings have taken place at Ravenshaw Court since he inherited it from the poor girl's father."

Kilgerrin frowned, brushed a hand through his tight-curling black hair. "When you first asked me to cultivate the girl . . ." He allowed the words to trail off into silence.

Lord MacQuarrie tilted his head, gazing at the young man. "Can such a heartless buck as yourself have fallen in love, Rob? The possibility of Cupid's darts penetrating such a thick hide seemed exceedingly remote when I first approached you for this task."

Watching the intricate pattern in the rug, Kilgerrin replied, "My reputation as a heartbreaker is greatly exaggerated. As you know, Lord Mac, I would have married three years since if—"

"Yes, yes, I know. She was a splendid fine girl, Rob, and I regret causing you to think of her now." He settled down into a chair. "I had forgotten."

"Despite my opinion of our esteemed Regent, I agreed to work with you," said Kilgerrin slowly, head still lowered. "It's because I have a certain loyalty to England, no matter what fat backside decorates the throne." He looked up now, blue eyes narrowed. "Yet the more I indulge in this . . . this clandestine work of ours, the more uneasy I feel. It's as though I were a Bow Street Runner who's become as corrupt as the criminals he hunts."

"The Runners are not all of them corrupt, Rob, and in the absence of any other sort of police force in our metropolis, they are much needed," said MacQuarrie. "I think no more of our illustrious Prince than you, but I much prefer his rule to that of Boney. Which is why I find myself involved in some very unsavory work from time to time." He leaned forward, knobby hands resting on his sharp knees. "Will you, Rob, continue to help us?"

After a long silent moment, Kilgerrin said, "I expect I'll encounter Alicia at Lady Westlake's ball tomorrow evening. That, by the way, is the only reason I can think of for attending such a predictably dull affair."

"Lady Westlake," said the other, slowly sighing out smoke. "I recall how decidedly handsome she was when I first met her, her name was Maude Sedgwick then. Had a waist no larger, I assure you, than this." He constructed a quite small circle with his two knobby hands, shedding ashes as he did. "The dear lady's girth has appreciated considerably since that remote day."

"Considerably, yes." Kilgerrin stood up, moved

to the empty fireplace, and ran his fingertips along the stone mantle. "You honestly believe Alicia is important, that what she may know can be of any help?"

"I must pursue many threads, Rob, in hope one of them at least will lead us out of the labyrinth," Lord MacQuarrie answered. "We have to know more of Boney's plans. What you and I do is only a small part of a much vaster operation."

Scowling, Kilgerrin said, "I can't help feeling, to borrow a favorite phrase of yours, it's not a gentlemanly way of conducting things."

"You're absolutely right, my boy," the older man agreed. "In many areas these days one can not afford to be a gentleman at all."

"I have wandered into one of those areas, I see."

"You and the girl, yes."

"I sometimes wish . . ."

"Yes?"

Shaking his head, Kilgerrin said, "Very well, I'll do what I have to."

Chapter 4

Everything glittered.

The light from the ballroom's dangling crystal chandeliers made the muslin and gossamer gowns of the young women glimmer, made their diamonds and pearls sparkle, made the scarlet-tuniced uniforms of the military officers glow. The dazzling light even made the spectacles of the anxious mothers and scowling chaperones gleam. And all the glitter and flash seemed to be spinning around and around as though the dancers were fragments of some gigantic exploding kaleidoscope.

"I'm certain I've forgotten something," whispered Queen Bess as she and Alicia reached the marble staircase and stood looking down the wide corridor into the glistening ballroom.

"Perhaps it's Dante," suggested Alicia, who was

clad in a high-waisted satin evening gown, with a single strand of matched pearls around her slim, graceful neck. "You're so used to hauling him around with you, Aunt."

"Nonsense, child, I wouldn't think of bringing the dear little creature to a ball," said her gaunt, white-faced aunt. "Not that Dante wouldn't be better company than a good many of the vapid ninnies I'll have to suffer through tonight. Why you haven't wed by now is quite incomprehensible. You had no less than five offers in your first season—"

"Oh, and three since. But you know, Aunt, two only wanted to marry me for my money, one could talk of nothing but horses—I think he was fonder of Midnight than of me—three were old and not at all amusing, and—"

"You seem to have tabulated them carefully. You may spare me the other two, since I am to be spared nothing else this evening."

Smiling, Alicia patted her aunt's thin arm. "I appreciate the sacrifice you're making for me."

"Careening through London at the indecent hour of near midnight, marching up an interminable stone staircase, sitting for endless hours in a stifling room and listening to a priceless collection of dolts and . . . ah, dear Lady Westlake, you are looking absolutely stunning this evening. The crowning glory of this simply lovely affair."

They'd reached the spot where the formidable Lady Westlake, all three hundred and eight pounds of her, stood greeting her arriving guests. Her face was blessed with numerous chins and wedged beneath several of them, their bright gems peering out like tiny glowing eyes, were lavish necklaces. The face itself was painted and powdered, the hair an

23

improbable yellow. "Dear Elizabeth," said their hostess, extending a few of her beringed sausage-shaped fingers, "you, too, seem in the best of health and appearance. For one of your years I am astounded to . . ."

Alicia allowed her attention to wander. Eyes slightly narrowed, she was scanning the waltzing crowd in the large ballroom which lay before her. There was one special person she sought, one handsome grinning face she hoped to see.

". . . not feeling well, Alicia, my dear?"

Obviously their enormous hostess was addressing her. Yes, and fat inquiring fingers were poking at her side. "No, no, Lady Westlake," Alicia managed to reply, tossing her auburn curls in a manner she trusted would convey complete ease, "I've never felt better."

"Pale," said Lady Westlake. "Yes, you appear decidedly pale, my dear."

"Perhaps it's the excitement."

"If I were you, and I doubt I could ever slim down to such a fawnlike shape as yours, Alicia, yet if I were you I'd talk to Dr. Marryat. He's such a brilliant man for . . ."

Alicia knew she was pale now, she could feel the color draining out of her pretty face. Why was it the very mention of that wizened little medical man made her feel so chill, almost frightened? She didn't care for him, granted. Yet a mere reference to most of those she was not altogether fond of didn't produce such an effect.

"Is he . . . is he here this evening?" the girl asked finally.

"Oh, no, the poor dear man is much too busy," replied Lady Westlake. "I fear at times he'll simply work himself into an early grave. He's been such a marvelous help to me, I can tell you. Somehow simply looking into his eyes makes one feel . . . Ah, but you'll want to be dancing, dear Alicia, and I have many more dear guests to attend to."

Dismissed, Alicia and her aunt proceeded toward the music-filled ballroom.

"You do appear ill," said Queen Bess, leaning her white face close to the girl's. "Perhaps it would be best if we—"

"Not at all, Aunt," Alicia assured her. "I am perfectly and absolutely fine. A prolonged conversation with Lady Westlake is enough to turn even the sturdiest campaigner pale."

"Some women grow worse with age. But Maude always was something of a sow. I well remember the year . . ."

The reminiscence never reached Alicia. She'd noticed the man she had been searching for with her eyes since arriving. He was standing near a Grecian-style pillar, very straight and tall, Very attractive in his dark clawhammer tails and breeches. His black hair appeared slightly windblown, and the familiar grin was riding on his lips.

Rob Kilgerrin sensed her gaze almost at once. He turned his face toward her, and his grin broadened into a pleased smile.

"Excuse me, Queen Bess," said Alicia, intruding on her aunt's autobiographical monologue. "I'm going to join a friend of—"

"Please, child, don't go galloping right up to a young man. It's brazen. Allow him to approach—"

"Well, I should normally do so, of course, but as I have almost made up my mind to marry Mr. Kilgerrin, I—"

"*Marry* him! Don't be absurd, child. Your uncle and I will decide that. And why hasn't he spoken to Tobias?"

"Mr. Kilgerrin has not yet proposed marriage—not to me, at any rate," Alicia explained. "Do lower your voice, Aunt, I want this all to be a surprise to him. Men in general prefer to think they have initiated these matters, I believe. But you really must excuse me. I believe Miss Smedley is looking particularly well tonight, so it is urgent that I speak to him before she does."

Smiling brilliantly, Alicia left her, made her way around the ballroom.

Kilgerrin was already en route to her.

They came together behind the broad scarlet-coated back of Major Whyte-Melville.

"Miss Kingsley," said Kilgerrin, "I was hoping you'd be—"

"So was I." She took his hand, smiled up at him as he gave her fingers a warm, comforting squeeze.

Kilgerrin laughed, shook his head, still holding fast to her hand. "What is it about you? I'm no sooner in your vicinity than all my glibness deserts me. Not ten minutes ago I was absolutely brilliant in the company of the uninspiring Miss Miller."

"Oh, I don't doubt that," said Alicia. "I've heard you're a brilliant flatterer, although I've never myself experienced it."

"No? I meant to inundate you with praise," he said. "Perhaps tonight I can make up for it."

"I enjoy you much better when you're merely yourself."

"Another dull fellow, merely myself."

"Not at all."

Nodding, Kilgerrin said, "Miss Copplestone is with you, I perceive."

"We are, for all practical purposes, inseparable. It is quite astonishing, considering how few relatives I have, how much time I spend in their presence."

He was studying the slim girl's face, and a frown touched his brow. "You seem, perhaps, a trifle distressed. Has she been causing you any trouble?"

"None. Unless you count occasional boredom as trouble. That lapdog of hers, the abominable Dante, is something else again. I'd gladly consign him to a fiery tour in the celebrated footsteps of his namesake."

Kilgerrin didn't smile. "You really are not . . . are you ill, Miss Kingsley?"

She laughed lightly, turning away to watch a country dance commence on the highly polished dance floor. "Not at all," she replied. "Although if one more person suggests it, I may grow ill simply to oblige."

"Forgive me," he said. "I am undoubtedly being clumsy. But it cannot be an indifferent matter to me, anything that touches your happiness."

"Pray don't apologize, Mr. Kilgerrin." She turned to face him. "The heartfelt solicitude of one's friends . . ." she lowered her eyes for a moment, then raised them to his. It was a gesture her admirers generally found irresistible. "I can assure you, though, I am feeling very well."

"There, that's better," he said, smiling. "That blush has brought considerable color to your cheeks."

Glancing up into his handsome face, the girl said, "You haven't given up your interest in boxing, I see."

He touched the slight bruise on his cheek. "A lucky blow struck by the Brighton Butcher."

"I gather you're still leading the life of an idle young man," she said. "Caught up in the London social whirl, taking time out now and then to trade punches with some brute or other."

For a few seconds his blue eyes avoided hers. "You've very accurately summed up my misspent days," he replied. "Yet I live in the hope the sincere love of a good woman will bring about an amazing reformation."

"I'm sure that can be arranged eventually."

"And now," he said, taking her bare arm, "I'd be most honored, Miss Kingsley, if you'd dance with me."

Yes, it was exactly as before. That particular warmth which flowed through her when Rob Kilgerrin took hold of her. "A splendid suggestion," she answered.

Chapter 5

The night was rich with stars, the after-midnight sky an incredibly clear black.

Alicia watched the heavens, one narrow hip resting against the marble railing of the terrace. "I really don't enjoy talking about it," she was saying.

"Forgive me," said Kilgerrin, who was standing close beside her. "My earlier impression was that you had nothing but fond and pleasant memories of Ravenshaw Court."

Her frown intensified. "Yes, I suppose I do," she said slowly, fingertips stroking the marble. "And yet, of late I . . ." She wanted to confide in him about the terrible dreams which had been haunting her, about the frightening night walks through the moonlit house in Darkside Court. She couldn't, somehow, bring herself to confide at all. Of all the people she knew, Rob Kilgerrin was the only one Alicia felt she could trust completely. Still she found she wasn't able to talk about the nightmares or her fears about herself.

"Something's bothering you." He touched her bare arm. "Has your Uncle Tobias done anything to—"

"Uncle Tobias?" The girl laughed. "Really, Mr. Kilgerrin, Uncle Toby is the furthest thing from an ogre I can imagine. He's an absent-minded, bumbling sort of person, really very much like some country squire out of a novel by Henry Fielding." She felt uncomfortable, though, while telling him this. Uncle Toby had always been kind to her, in his own vague and preoccupied way. Why did talking about him lately unsettle her so?

"You don't see much of Tobias Copplestone these days?"

The girl replied, "Aunt Elizabeth and I have visited him twice in the year that we've been in London."

"And he remains at Ravenshaw most of the time?"

"Uncle Toby is always to be found there, so far as I am aware, Rob. There are the tenants to keep track of, various bits of Ravenshaw business to attend to." She turned to look at him. "Why are you showing such an interest in poor old Uncle Toby?"

The reflected starlight flashed out of her eyes for an instant. "Nothing more than an interest in you prompts my interest in him," Kilgerrin lied. "I'm like a poet who finds even the minutest detail of his lady's life a topic of overwhelming interest."

She smiled, glancing out at the shadowy garden beyond the broad terrace. "Then am I to expect

30

to see "An Ode to His Mistress's Doddering Uncle" in the pages of, perhaps, *The Examiner* some day soon?"

"Not until I put the finishing touches on the sonnet I'm penning about your aunt's lapdog," he answered, grinning. He placed a hand on her shoulder, held her with eyes that were suddenly serious. "Alicia, may I speak freely?" It was the first time he had addressed her by her Christian name. She thought he wasn't aware he had done so.

"I'll give to serious statements almost as much attention as I do to jests." Alicia smiled up at him. "I trust, however, you're not planning to become very somber. My list of somber acquaintances is much too long as it is."

"Miss Kingsley . . . Alicia . . ." He said nothing more. Instead he pulled her, almost roughly, to him and kissed her.

She had speculated on what his kiss would be like and, as she chided herself afterwards, she ought to have paid close attention to all the details. Instead she lost all track of time, of the stars above and the shadow-filled garden below. She felt incredibly warm and timeless.

Finally, it seemed a long time later, she became aware of something besides the strong, comforting pressure of Rob Kilgerrin's arms around her. The silky black sky returned, the formal garden, the bright, color-filled ballroom at their side.

"Rob," she breathed softly.

He moved slightly away from her, his strong hands holding on to hers. "There's something I think, perhaps, I must tell . . ."

He was interrupted by a fairly loud smacking sound in the dark garden below the terrace.

"Sir, I suspect you are trying to take advantage of me!"

"By Hecate, madam, were I attempting to seduce you, there'd be not a single doubt in your mind!"

From behind a high trimmed hedge emerged a thin lady. She was, they noticed as she came striding toward them, somewhat past the first blush of youth. Her sunken cheeks glowed with an unnatural redness and her golden hair sat somewhat askew on her skull. The lacy bodice of her satin evening gown was in a state of moderate dissarray. "That bloated popinjay," she muttered when she barged by them to go slamming into the bright-lit ballroom. "I should have known better than to take a stroll with a satirist."

Kilgerrin was gazing down into the garden, his grin widening. "I recognize the voice of the offender," he told Alicia.

While the two young people watched, a huge form took shape beside a lifesize marble statue of Venus. The man weighed, at the very least, three hundred pounds. He wore a bottle-green frock coat, a vast white waistcoat, and knee breeches of an emerald hue. Perched on his huge head was an old-fashioned and not overly convincing wig of sandy-colored hair. He might be fifty or he might be sixty, surely somewhere between those two milestones on the short road of life. His face, in the thin moonlight, somewhat resembled that of a gingerbread man. It was big and round, the eyes and mouth seemed to have been pushed into the dough before it was baked. The nose was an afterthought, an impressive tomato-like object which garnished the whole ensemble.

"Damme," he rumbled to himself in his booming voice. "I'd sooner take a broomstick to bed than that slattern. By Hecate, a man noted for impeccable taste and artistic discrimination accused of attempting the honor, such as it is, of the likes of Annabelle Van Der—Ah, good evening, Rob!" He'd become aware of his audience, touched two pudgy fingers to his wide, high forehead in a lazy salute.

"You appear to have been misunderstood by the Widow Van Der Boom," Kilgerrin observed.

"I was merely admiring the lace on the dear lady's gown." Setting up a bagpipe of a wheezing, the immense man came stomping through the garden in their direction. He lumbered with the aid of a sturdy cudgel functioning as a cane, tromping over flower beds and across formal paths like some fearful juggernaut.

"Alicia Kingsley, this sudden apparition is none other than the notorious Thomas Rowdybranch," said Kilgerrin when his enormous friend was on the marble terrace with them.

The girl bowed slightly, smiling. "You're a very gifted artist, Mr. Rowdybranch."

"I'm not an artist at all, young lady." Rowdybranch gave a snort. "Merely a clever penman, one step above a forger. In fact, my talent could safely be ensconced in the orifice of . . . Yow!" The fat man had been gesturing with his stick and had managed to thwack his right foot with the heavy gnarled stick.

The foot, they now both noticed, was heavily enveloped in bandages.

"Gout again?" inquired Rob Kilgerrin.

"So the eminent undertaker's friend, Dr. William Emerson, claims," replied Rowdybranch. "He maintains I suffer this blasted plague because of high living and excessive debauchery." Another snort. "How could any creature live higher than a Cockney birdseller on the pitiful sums my caricatures earn me? As for lustful adventures, well, you've only just now witnessed how successful I am at that sort of thing."

"Your drawings really are very telling," said Alicia. "My aunt, of course, disapproves of your work very strongly. Yet I've managed to amass quite a collection."

The artist studied the girl more carefully. "Here, by Hecate, is a most perceptive young person, Rob my boy," he announced. "Unusual to find you in the company of anyone with a brain larger than an East Indian nutmeg."

"Continued association with you, Thomas, has apparently sharpened my wits," Kilgerrin replied. "I honestly have to believe I've caught good taste from you the way one might catch the pox."

Making a rumbling sound, Rowdybranch said, "Would that I could infect a few others. That suet pudding who attempts to rule Britain between visits to his bawds and—Gadzooks! You're Alicia Kingsley."

The girl was startled by his sudden surprised bellow. "Why . . . yes, I am."

"Which is the reason for my introducing her as such," put in Kilgerrin.

"My wits were addled when first we met," admitted the huge artist. He took a ponderous step backwards and studied the girl with his large head tilted to one side.

She lowered her eyes. "I hope you're not intending to include me in one of your etchings, sir."

"Not at all, not at all," he assured her in his rumbling voice. "I happen to have been, in an unfortunately casual way, acquainted with your late father and mother. There is, as you obviously must be aware, a very striking resemblance between you and your mother."

"So I've determined from the few drawings of her I've seen," said Alicia quietly. "She died when I was quite young."

"The best people are always taken from us too soon," said Rowdybranch. "It's only rogues and rascals and jades who seem immortal." He reached out a huge hand to take hold of Kilgerrin by the elbow. "Rob, my boy, if Miss Kingsley will excuse us for a brief interval, I'd like a few words with you."

Kilgerrin said, "Well, the truth of the matter is, Thomas, you emerged from the foliage at a rather—"

"Like a cross between a sea nymph and a leviathan rising from the ocean waves?" said Rowdybranch. "I fear I made my debut in the midst of some tender scene between you twain. There's so little real affection in this world, I'm sorry to have interrupted what—"

"I really must go soothe my aunt," put in Alicia now. "You can rescue me once you and Mr. Rowdybranch have had your discussion, Rob." Smiling at both of them, the girl withdrew.

The artist waited until she was back inside the swirl of the ballroom. "I do not at all like this, my lad," he said in a relatively subdued voice.

"Alicia's a wonderful girl, I can't see why you'd object to—"

"Damn, Rob, don't go playing the cunning politician with me," warned the mammoth Rowdybranch, his grip on the young man's arm tightening. "I know what's going on in London. Everything that's public knowledge and a good deal that's not. You're working for MacQuarrie and his corps of spies."

"You must realize why I—"

"Yes, yes, God save the King and all that. Three rousing cheers for Britannia," said Rowdybranch. "Can't expect you to have as much sense as I do and see that all governments are nothing more than carbuncles on the backside of society. We'll let the political philosophy lecture pass, my boy. The important point I wish to make is this . . . I advise you very strongly not to lead that splendid young woman astray!"

"Astray? Listen to me, Thomas, I love Alicia and—"

"Love are you calling it, Rob? Yet wasn't it Lord Mac, that smoke-belching conniver, who put you up to courting her?"

Kilgerrin didn't answer. He pulled free of the older man's grip, walked several feet away.

Rowdybranch came gallumping after him. "Ah, I see," he wheezed. "Assigned to spy, he stays to woo. Very touching."

"Damn you!" Kilgerrin whirled to face him. "I do love her! I admit I was . . . that it began as nothing more than a task. Now, however, Thomas, I swear to you, I . . ." He let out an exasperated sigh. "I don't know, everything is in a very unhappy state."

Rowdybranch told him, "You'll have to make up your mind which you are, I'd say. It's unlikely you can be both a government agent and the lover of a girl like Alicia Kingsley."

"It's not exactly so simple," protested the young

man, running a hand through his curling dark hair. "We are at war, after all."

"Are you raising the shadow of Bonaparte to justify what you're up to, my lad? More scoundrels sail under the flag of war than ever ran up the Jolly Roger." He tapped the terrace stones with his cudgel.

"I cannot be like you, Thomas, above the battle. Sitting up in that atelier of yours like some god on Olympus, looking down at the pathetic mortals far below you."

"By Hecate, my studio is only on the first floor, over the print shop. Not a very lofty or godlike vantage point, Rob," he insisted. He took hold of his young friend's arm once again. "I have been hearing certain things about the girl. You must realize I have far better informants working for me than your Lord Mac or any of the Regent's toadies."

"What do you mean, what have you heard?"

"Nothing, have no fear, to sully her character," said Rowdybranch. He stroked his nearly spherical nose with his free hand. "Now I've seen her up close again after many a long year, I'm inclined to undertake a more active part in all this."

"If you know anything which might—"

"My boy, I find myself usually awash with gossip, blather, facts, truths, half-truths, and libels. I attract such stuff like a lodestone draws filings to it," said the artist. "When I've done a bit more astute gleaning, I'll contact you. In the meantime, it goes without saying, you are always welcome to call at my studio above the print shop in St. James's Street."

"Yes, thank you, Thomas, I shall," said Kilgerrin, frowning. "But isn't there something further you can tell me now?"

Rowdybranch shook his head, causing his spurious hair to do a little hop. "Not now," he said. "I'll leave you here to have a bit of a wrestle with your conscience. Myself, I'll reenter the ball and try my luck at wrestling with one of the stunning ladies I discovered earlier."

Chapter 6

The sound of hoofbeats filled the world.

The thundering sound of pursuit through the night forest was all around Alicia as she galloped away from Ravenshaw Court on her ebony stallion.

They wanted to kill her.

She was certain of that, and her heart beat so violently it shook her entire body.

Rushing down that same shadowy road again, the chill darkness almost clutching at her. They wanted to kill her, she must get away.

But who were they? Whom was she running away from? She'd never done it before, yet tonight she had the irresistible impulse to look behind her, to find out who her pursuers were.

A moment rushed by as she worked up her nerve. Her powerful mount pounded on across the night.

Alicia turned her head.

It was death. A scarlet-cloaked figure with a gleaming, grinning skull for a head was riding at the head of the gang of pursuers. When he saw her staring at him, his mouth flapped open and he began to laugh.

The sunlight caressed her, touching her face. Alicia blinked, rubbing her eyes.

She found herself in her bedroom, standing at the window. The day had already commenced, and a milk cart rolled by, its ancient dappled mare clopping slowly over the paving stones.

"Another dream," the girl realized, pressing her fingertips to the smooth flesh above her breasts. "And I went perambulating once more."

She continued to watch Darkside Square come to life. At No. 79 old Mr. Ferris himself was on his bony knees scrubbing off his front steps. A task he often performed and one, according to Queen Bess, which marked him as a great eccentric. The wicker baker's cart appeared, pushed by the usual pudgy one-armed boy. At No. 86 the youngest DeLacy boy came sneaking out the delivery door to go scurrying into the tiny park which made a green triangle at the far end of the square. The boy, who was an extremely unappealing ten-year-old, yanked a slingshot from a rear pocket of his breeches and took up a position behind a box hedge. His puffy little eyes were on the sparrows gathering on the still dewy grass.

"He's such a terrible shot," reflected Alicia, "that our feathered friends should be quite safe."

Leaving the window, the girl returned to her high-post bed and sat on its edge. She hugged herself once, noticing gooseflesh forming on her arms.

Try as she might, she couldn't control these

40

dreams and the night excursions which often accompanied them. Fortunately this latest nightmare hadn't awakened her Aunt Elizabeth. The next one, though, might.

"I . . . I won't let them take me to Dr. Marryat!"

But her aunt would try to drag her to the wizened little doctor, unless the dreams and all the rest of it ceased. Alicia had to get help from someone else, or at least must confide in someone else.

An image of herself in Rob Kilgerrin's arms filled her thoughts. She saw herself swirling around the ballroom floor two nights ago, happy, warm, and . . . yes, in love.

"You do love him," Alicia told herself.

That was true, yes. She felt about the handsome Rob as she'd felt about no other man in her twenty-two years of life. She felt certain she could trust him and that he would do anything to help her.

Yet Alicia hesitated about telling him what was troubling her. Two nights ago, when Rob had shown concern over how she might be feeling, the girl had been on the verge of confiding. But she found she couldn't.

Why?

Was she ashamed of what was happening to her? Did she fear he would turn against her if he suspected there was something wrong with her, that she might be going mad?

No, it wasn't that. It was . . .

Alicia shook her head. She could never quite put her finger on it, the motive for her reticence. Trying to get at it was like chasing some very illusive little creature through the intricacies of a labyrinth.

A tapping started up on the door of her room, followed soon after by a persistent yapping.

"Yes, Aunt?" the girl called in the direction of the door.

It opened a few inches, and Dante came charging in, yelping profusely.

"Hush, hush, you wicked little devil." Queen Bess came striding into the room.

"He's no doubt yowling because he's overjoyed to see me," suggested the girl as she fended off Dante's attempts to approach her with her bare foot.

"Why aren't you dressed, child?" asked her aunt, who was.

"Chiefly because I've only just awakened."

"We're shopping this morning, remember?" reminded Queen Bess. "Then we must pay a call on dear Mrs. Yates in Fitzroy Square. Their new townhouse is a momentous eyesore, but she's a delightful person nonetheless."

"I prefer the house to her," murmured the girl.

"What's that, child?"

"I was mentioning, Aunt, that if you and Dante will withdraw, I'll attend to transforming myself into a completely presentable young belle."

"Yes, yes, and do hurry." Bending, with some creaking and muttering, the old woman scooped up the dog and tucked him under her arm, from which position he glowered and growled at Alicia. "It should prove to be a most amusing day."

Actually, as Alicia well knew, it would be a very dull day. As were most of the days which didn't contain Rob Kilgerrin. Since she wasn't due to see him again until next Saturday, there was nothing Alicia could do but dress herself and make the most of Queen Bess's little excursion.

Which is what she did.

Chapter 7

But finally she did tell him.

It was a warm, sultry night, and they were walking along one of the many tree-lined lanes which crosshatched Vauxhall Gardens. The branches of the tall trees were festooned with globes of light, and Alicia felt as though she and Rob Kilgerrin had been transported completely off the prosiac Earth and were strolling, alone and content, far out in the star-studded sky.

The noise and music of the vast amusement garden faded as they walked hand in hand. There were few other strollers on this particular leafy path.

One of the globular oil lamps in the branches high above sputtered suddenly and died, sending up a thin spume of sooty smoke.

"Are there," Kilgerrin inquired, "any further Vauxhall delights you wish to enjoy?"

Laughing, the girl shook her head. "I can think of none. We've heard the orchestra in the pavilion play the latest tunes from Vienna, we've been assaulted by Madame Roberta's rendition of what was allegedly an Italian air, and we've gasped appreciatively while Signore Busino performed his death-defying dance on the tight-rope."

"Well, then it appears as though we . . . ah, look." He halted, pointing skyward.

An enormous scarlet flower was blossoming in the velvety night sky. A muffled explosion was heard, and seconds later two giant splashes of gold filled the blackness high above them. More explosions, more pinwheels of crimson, gold, marine, and emerald.

"Fireworks," exclaimed Alicia, delighted, "I love them."

"We all do," said Kilgerrin. "So long as they aren't produced by cannons and French troops."

Nodding, she said, "Yes, what I enjoy, I suppose, is seeing the spectacle of battle with none of its dangers."

Kilgerrin said, "This is bordering on a serious conversation, Alicia, the sort of thing not allowed in this locale." He started to move forward.

She held him back. "Rob, I want . . . to talk to you about a matter of some concern."

He stepped back from her, placing his hands, gently, on her slim shoulders. "I hope you've not chosen this night to inform me you've decided to see no more of me."

"I would never come to a conclusion like that," she said, softly.

44

A frown touched his face. "I have sensed you've been troubled lately, Alicia."

"That's what I believe we had better discuss."

Taking her arm, he led her along the pathway until they came to a rustic bench in a small clearing. "We can sit here and talk if you'd like," he invited.

"Yes, that would be fine."

Up above, three rockets scrawled sparkling red trails across the night.

"Is there someone who's causing you trouble, Alicia?" He took her hand.

"No, I'm afraid the person who's troubling me is myself."

"Are you . . . ill?"

She shook her head. "Not physically, I don't believe," she answered. "As for my mental state, I'm not as certain."

Kilgerrin grinned. "Come now, Alicia, there are few women in London in better control of their mental faculties than you," he assured her. "You're one of the most level-headed and sensible girls I know."

"That may be," she said, "yet for many weeks I've been suffering from the most violent sort of nightmares." She glanced away from him, at the dark moss all around them.

"Bad dreams visit everyone."

"Not merely bad dreams," she persisted. "It is the same horrible dream again and again. Worse, Rob, I've taken to walking in my sleep. I often awake to find myself in some other part of the house. And I never have any recollection of how I got there. I fall asleep in my own bed, but I awaken on the staircase or at my window."

His grip on her hand tightened. "You might hurt yourself," he said. "You might fall."

"Yes, something might happen to my body," she said. "What is more unsettling, though, is what's happening to my mind."

"This dream," he said. "Can you tell me about that?"

"Yes . . . in the dream I am always riding away from Ravenshaw Court. Night after night there's some sort of furious chase. I'm riding Midnight, my favorite horse. Behind me, Rob, there's a pack of men riding fast, and I always know they mean to kill me if they catch me. I know, too, I must escape from Ravenshaw. If I don't, I'll die."

"Yet in the waking world you have no such feelings about the place."

"No, I . . ." She paused, growing pale.

"What's wrong?"

"Nothing exactly, Rob . . . I felt a sudden wave of dread. Some warning inside me about Ravenshaw Court." She shook her head from side to side several times. "I don't know . . . I seem to be certain that should I return there, I'll die."

"Did something happen at Ravenshaw?" he asked, eyes on her pale, anxious face. "Some unpleasant incident?"

"No, there . . . Yes, it . . ." She stopped, pressed her hand against her chest. "I had only pleasant times there."

He said, "Perhaps not."

"What do you mean?"

"It seems likely some upsetting incident did take place there, Alicia. Something you witnessed and forgot, but may now be trying to recall."

"I'd most certainly remember any terrible experience I'd had at Ravenshaw."

"The thing might have happened years ago, when you were a child."

"My childhood was a very happy one," she said. "Except for my mother's death."

Kilgerrin said, "And in more recent times your Uncle Tobias has done nothing to frighten you or—"

"Uncle Toby? Believe me, Rob, as I tried to persuade you before, he's the most gentle and well-meaning of men."

"Yes, so you've said."

"You sound as though you don't quite believe my appraisal of Uncle Toby's character."

"I believe you think him nothing more than a harmless old country gentlemen," said Kilgerrin.

"You've asked me about my uncle before. Is there—"

"No, Alicia, I know of nothing to besmirch his character," said Kilgerrin, not quite truthfully. "Since I'm concerned for you, I'm interested in those who comprise your circle."

Alicia stood. "I'd like to walk back to the pavilion."

He rose. "Are you angry because I've been asking you all these questions?"

"It's only because I feel suddenly very tired," she said. "If you won't hate me, Rob, I think I'd best return home."

"Of course, even though it will pretty thoroughly blight the evening." He held out his arm.

"There'll be many more evenings for us," she promised, taking his arm.

As they began walking back in the direction of

47

the crowds and laughter, he said, "We are going to have to do something about those dreams of yours."

"Lock me away in some bedlam," she said. "That might be the simplest solution."

"Alicia, don't even jest about your mental state. There is nothing wrong with you," he said. "I do suggest, however, you might benefit from consulting a medical friend of mine."

She told him, "Not yet."

"He's a very good man, an expert in the very sort of—"

"Not yet," she repeated firmly. "I do appreciate your concern, Rob. I feel all the better for having talked this out with you. For now, I'm not ready to discuss it with anyone else."

"Letting too much time pass isn't—"

"Blimey! Look who it is," said a gruff voice.

Approaching them along the lane of tall trees was the Brighton Butcher, arm in arm with a brightly attired young lady.

"Good evening," said Kilgerrin, slowing.

"It's as I was explainin' to Floss here, gov," said the boxer as the two couples passed each other. "You see a lot of swells here at Vauxhall. That you do."

"That you do," agreed Rob Kilgerrin.

"And who was that imposing gentleman?" asked Alicia.

"A professor of my acquaintance."

"Indeed? He didn't strike me as very academic."

"He specializes in pugilism," answered Kilgerrin, grinning. "Thus his manner is not quite as polished as that of a professor of the classics."

"Then he's the one who's responsible for the bruises which occasionally decorate your face."

"He is."

They were in the midst of people now, couples from all stations of life, the highest to the lowest. The crowd circled the bright, light-decked pavilion, where the orchestra was now rendering a medley of martial music. To the left were the boxes filled with dining, drinking patrons of Vauxhall Gardens. Much ham and beef was being consumed, along with large sloshing quantities of the formidable punch for which the pleasure gardens were famed.

Alicia and Kilgerrin moved through the crowd and out an arched exitway. There were a few other couples slowly moving toward the dock for the trip back across the Thames.

In a low voice Alicia said, "There's one other thing I meant to confide in you, Rob."

"Yes?" He leaned his handsome head close to hers.

"I'm very fond of you," she told him.

Kilgerrin didn't immediately respond. Then finally he said, "And I of you."

She wondered why he had hesitated.

Chapter 8

A crisp afternoon wind was blowing across St. James's Street as Rob Kilgerrin crossed the cobblestones and aimed himself at the door of the printseller's shop. He lifted one hand and held on to the brim of his beaver hat to keep the wind from snatching it away.

The shop was housed in a thin three-story building, mahogany-brown in color. Its door was painted a bright yellow and sported a brass knocker fashioned in the shape of a leering satyr's head. Painted boldly in crimson letters on the lintel above the narrow doorway were the words *Mrs. Draper, Printseller*. The shop's bay window bellied out over the sidewalk and was filled completely with rows of prints of Thomas Rowdybranch's latest attacks on the Prince Regent, the peers of the realm, and the lords of creation and such other targets which had come into his ken and caused him vexation. Some of the satirical engravings were black and others, the more costly, were gorgeously hand-colored and seemed to glow in the afternoon sunlight. A half-dozen potential customers were gathered in front of the bulging window, gazing at Rowdybranch's newest works. One gentleman in a fawn greatcoat had apparently begun laughing at one of the drawings while inhaling snuff and was now suffering a paroxysm which mingled guffawing, sneezing, and choking. An off-duty chimney sweep was helpfully slapping the gentleman on his broad back, succeeding thus far only in imprinting several sooty handprints on the fabric of the greatcoat.

Kilgerrin, skirting the crowd, entered Mrs. Draper's shop.

There were two mahogany counters, forming a sort of L. On the walls behind the counters rose nests of narrow drawers, containing Rowdybranch's past satirical triumphs. A glass showcase to the immediate left of the entryway displayed several copies of his latest work, a brilliantly colored drawing of Napoleon in the guise of a cherub.

Mrs. Draper herself was behind one of the counters, rolling a print into a cylinder and wrapping it in green paper before tying it with green cord. She was a thin woman, wearing a lace mobcap on her gray hair. After handing the wrapped print to the clerical-seeming customer, she smiled at Kilgerrin. "You'll have to be nimble today, sir," she told him.

"Is that the sort of mood he's in?"

"One has to be as artful a dodger as the chap at Bartholomew Fair," the proprietress advised Kilgerrin. "He's much inclined to the tossing about of things. Nearly brained me with his teapot not an hour ago and was eyeing his engraving tools most speculatively when I fled his lair." She sighed, folding her thin arms across her narrow chest. "I suppose that's the price one has to pay for sharing one's roof with genius."

"There are, I've heard, geniuses who don't toss teapots," replied Kilgerrin with a grin. He crossed the narrow shop, heading for a curtained exit at its rear. "I'll risk bearding him."

"Good luck to you, sir."

Kilgerrin climbed a shadowy, twisting wooden staircase. As he neared the top a blend of scents came wafting down at him. Prominent was the sharp odor of acid, the stuff Rowdybranch used on his copperplate engravings. There was also the somewhat subtler smell of rum. He tapped on the half-open door and waited.

"No use trying to make up for the harm you've done me, madam."

"Thomas, hold your fire," Kilgerrin called out.

"Ah, the dashing young espier," rumbled the immense artist. "Come in, Rob, my boy."

Rowdybranch was enthroned—that was the word which flashed into Kilgerrin's mind—on a massive balloon-back armchair, his gouty foot resting precariously on a forlorn ottoman. A drawing board rested on his ample lap. Beside him on a taboret a green jug of rum nested among a scatter of engraving tools.

The studio itself was a large room, alternately light and dark. Sunlight came slanting down through a spotless skylight, but the corners of the room were benighted and piles of books, prints, and not quite identifiable objects lurked there. Kilgerrin thought he spotted a stuffed owl, new since his last visit, huddled in one dusty corner. Close to Rowdybranch's slightly lopsided throne was the small press he used for running off test proofs. Two jugs of nitric acid and three of varnish sat nearby the press.

Rowdybranch was sketching with a stubby stick of charcoal on a large wrinkled sheet of white paper. "Some men are haunted by visions of lovely lasses they've only caught brief glimpses of in Florentine cathedrals," he said in his throaty voice. "I find myself, by way of contrast, taken today with the Regent's backside." He held up the sketches he'd been making.

Kilgerrin laughed. "A very good likeness," he said, "speaking from my limited experience with the subject."

"Oh, so? I fancied you and Lord Mac paid frequent homage to the object in question."

"Thomas," said Kilgerrin, moving closer to his friend, "I've explained to you before why I choose to serve—"

"Yes, to be sure, my boy." The artist leaned to set aside the drawing board. "Now then, if we're through singing hymns in praise of God and country, I have something to discuss with you. I was, in point of fact, about to attempt cajoling dear Mrs. Draper into allowing her weak-witted assistant, the redoubtable Miss Hill, to take a message to you."

Kilgerrin seated himself in Rowdybranch's only other chair, a ramshackle cane-bottom. "All of your work, Thomas, attacks folly and vice," he said evenly. "I assume, therefore, you believe the world can be improved and made better for those of us inhabiting it. Why do you chide me when—"

"Ha!" boomed the fat man, his gout-ridden foot jiggling on its perch. "Are you advancing the dubious notion of the perfectability of man?" he inquired, laughing more heartily. "I assure you, Rob, I've never sought any such grail. No, Rowdybranch merely chronicles what he sees, with no other purpose than to amuse. Laughter, my boy, is actually the only weapon we have to keep ourselves sane in this shabby hurlyburly."

"Very well, I won't debate the issue." Kilgerrin leaned forward. "Why were you going to send for me?"

Shifting his massive bulk, Rowdybranch fished a scrap of pasteboard out of the crammed pocket of his smoking jacket. "I am very much interested, as I mentioned to you at dear Lady Westlake's stupefying ball the other evening, in your Alicia Kingsley." He commenced sketching something on the scrap of paper.

"As am I, Thomas."

"So you claim," mumbled Rowdybranch while he drew. "Torn 'twixt love and duty, came to scoff and stayed to pray, sundry other attitudinizing cant."

"I do *love* her! Why can't you—"

"Know the owner of this unprepossessing phiz?"

Kilgerrin's eyes narrowed to study the quick charcoal portrait his friend was holding toward him. "Yes, I've seen him about London on occasion," he answered. "His name is Dr. Noah Marryat . . . we have reason to suspect he may be disloyal."

"Oh, he is that for a certainty, my boy." Rowdybranch turned the pasteboard over and rested it again on one massive knee. "He is also, my ferrets inform me, the cohort of this worthy gent." He held up a new portrait in his thick fingers.

"Lord Cranford? But he's a member of the cabinet, we've never heard a word spoken against him."

"Chiefly because Cranford is a deal cleverer than most of those who labor in His Majesty's Secret Service, my boy."

"Do you have definite proof that—"

"At the moment I have proof of nothing," said the fat artist, flinging the caricature to the already cluttered floor. "I operate on rumor and innuendo, plus some very reliable hunches. By stitching all these bits and pieces together, Rob, I quite often construct for myself a living, breathing homunculus."

Kilgerrin said, "Then let's return to the topic of Dr. Marryat. What does he have to do with Alicia?"

"Do you know if she sees him, in a professional way?"

"She doesn't. In fact, she has a very pronounced aversion to the fellow."

Rubbing at his bulbous nose, Rowdybranch said, "With good reason, I'll wager."

"Has he done something to Alicia, in the past?" Kilgerrin asked, half-rising from his chair.

"Be calm, my boy." The artist made a sit-down motion with one plump hand. "This is not yet the time for action. We're still harvesting and have not reached the point where we'll separate the wheat from the tares. What you are most in need of at this time is wise counsel."

"Which you intend to provide?"

Chuckling, Rowdybranch answered, "Exactly. My lecture shall begin with some interesting anecdotes from the life and times of Noah Marryat."

Chapter 9

After dinner the guests were required to adjourn to the spacious drawing room for an hour of music provided by their hostess's three very marriageable daughters.

The final performer of the evening was Miss Maude Besant, a slender, taffy-haired girl of nineteen.

Midway through the girl's attack on Handel, Alicia leaned closer to Rob Kilgerrin, who shared a tufted loveseat with her. She whispered, "Who is that rawboned gentleman with the aquiline features? He seems to be somewhat interested in us."

Kilgerrin didn't need to glance across the room at the sharp-nosed man who sat in a dark armchair near the wide fireplace. He was already aware of the covert scrutiny. "I thought you were introduced before dinner," he answered in a low voice. "He's Lord Cranford, member of the cabinet and in all ways a very important figure in political circles."

"Oh, yes, of course. I've heard of him, and I believe your friend Mr. Rowdybranch has honored him with a caricature more than once," she said, thoughtfully. "Why, do you suppose, is such an astute statesman taking such an interest in the pair of us?"

"I imagine he's actually only interested in studying you, Alicia." Kilgerrin didn't wish to share with her the hints about Cranford which Rowdybranch had passed on to him three days before. "A good many other moths have been drawn to your flame."

She shook her head. "I don't sense any admiration in that furtive gaze. There is only a cold sort of appraisal, almost as though I were a slave on the block and he a prospective buyer."

"Lord Cranford is not noted for exceptional warmth," said Kilgerrin. "Now we'd best curtail our conversation until the conclusion of the entertainment. I believe Mrs. Besant is working up to cast a disapproving scowl in our direction."

Although he'd attempted to dismiss the subject of Lord Cranford's interest, Kilgerrin was very much concerned. Why was the sharp-featured politician eyeing the girl in such a speculative way? Kilgerrin strived to shrug the matter off, trying to convince himself Rowdybranch's remarks had simply made him overly suspicious.

Something nudged him in the side.

"The concert is over," Alicia informed him.

Kilgerrin, who'd been lost in thought, blinked. "So it is." He sent a polite smile in the general direction of Mrs. Besant.

"There's something I never thought I'd see," remarked Alicia, her face near to his. "A false smile on your lips."

"Ah, but I have a whole repertoire of them," he responded. "Suitable for a wide variety of social occasions. Actually, though, Honoria is not a bad pianist."

"That was Maude we just heard."

"Was it now?"

"Yes," laughed Alicia. "And may I inquire what has you so distracted this evening?"

"Very well, I confess I was thinking of you when I should have been paying close attention to which Miss Besant was thumping the piano when."

Alicia lowered her head slightly. "An acceptable excuse," she said. "Let us hope dear Mrs. Besant will accept it."

"I fear our hostess suspects I'm no longer a candidate for the hand of even one of her fair daughters."

"I say," said someone who they now both realized had been standing over them for several seconds. He was a brusk, broad-chested man in a scarlet-tuniced uniform. "Didn't get the opportunity, Miss Kingsley, to introduce meself at dinner. Hope you won't think me forward for so doing now."

"Not at all, Major."

"Happen to be Major George Drumgoole," he announced, giving his substantial mustache a fluffing flick and clicking his booted heels together. "Had the pleasure, distinct pleasure, of being an acquaintance of your late father. Splendid chap, you know. I say, you've turned into a quite handsome gal. Yes."

"Thank you, Major," said Alicia, rising. "Did you ever visit us at Ravenshaw Court? I'm afraid I don't recall you, and I'm certain I would if we'd met."

"Knew your father only in town, we were both members of the Fagin Club and Barbican's, you know."

"I believe," said Kilgerrin, as he stood, "I'll compliment Mrs. Besant on the abundant musical talents of her offspring."

"I say, I haven't barged into a nest of love birds, have I now?"

"Not at all, Major Drumgoole," Kilgerrin assured him, moving away from him and Alicia.

"Lovely, absolutely lovely," remarked Mrs. Besant, holding out a hand gleaming with rings and brooches. "Alicia is most certainly turning into a beauty."

"She made that transformation long since," corrected Kilgerrin. He took the proffered hand and pressed it.

When the woman spoke, her high-piled hair tended to jiggle. "What an absolutely killing couple you make, Rob," she continued. "I envy Alicia, though I sometimes fear, Robbie dear, you are much too restless and heedless. I do hear the most astonishing tales of your escapades."

"Really? I can't imagine why, since I lead an almost cloistered life."

"They do say, Robbie dear, you've even entered the boxing ring to fight with some very brutal fellows. I find it most difficult to believe."

"I'd advise you not to credit such idle talk," Kilgerrin told her. "I did want to tell you how much I enjoyed hearing your marvelous set of daughters perform this evening."

"Poppycock, Robbie dear," said Mrs. Besant with a hearty laugh. "You saw and heard nothing but Alicia from the moment you crossed my threshold."

"Ah, good evening, Kilgerrin." Lord Cranford was standing now with his back to the fireplace quite nearby.

A fact Kilgerrin had taken into consideration when he went up to pay his compliments to their hostess. Bowing to Mrs. Besant, he turned to face the hawk-nosed statesman. "One wouldn't have thought the country's affairs would allow you any time for society, Lord Cranford."

"Precious little," replied Cranford in his thin nasal voice. "Had I the leisure of fellows such as yourself I doubt not I'd lead an altogether different sort of life. Unfortunately, my duties allow me little time to pay court to charming young ladies such as Miss Kingsley."

"Are you acquainted with her?"

"Alas, no." Cranford smiled a small rueful smile. "I do believe I met her father once or twice."

"And her uncle, Tobias Copplestone?"

"I have never had that pleasure, no," he said. "I do hope, by the way, Kilgerrin, you'll forgive my rather rude conduct this evening. I fear I found our musical interlude quite boring and your Miss Kingsley extremely fascinating."

Kilgerrin studied the aquiline face. "No doubt Miss Kingsley will forgive you," he said finally.

"A work of art, after all, must expect to attract admirers."

"Yes, obviously," said Kilgerrin. "Now I feel obliged to rescue her before Major Drumgoole completely inundates her with military anecdotes." With a very slight bow, he left Lord Cranford.

While crossing the room toward Alicia, Kilgerrin thought, "Cranford never admired a fellow creature in all his bleak life. His interest in Alicia has nothing to do with affection."

Chapter 10

They drifted silently through the thick gray fog. It muffled the sounds of the carriage wheels and the horses' hooves.

Inside Alicia rested her head against Kilgerrin's chest. "You agree with me, then?"

He stroked the auburn curls at her temple. "Incredible as it seems, I believe his interest in you has nothing to do with admiration."

"Whatever his reasons, I'd rather Lord Cranford turned his attentions elsewhere."

"You're absolutely certain you can think of no cause for his interest?"

"None, Rob." When she shook her head, it brushed gently against his chest.

"We'll see if we can't avoid him henceforward."

"You seem extremely agitated by this," she

told him. "I admit I'd rather he hadn't chosen to gaze at me all evening, yet the man is not exactly a deep-dyed villain. He holds a most respectable position in the government."

"There may be another side to his character."

Alicia lifted her head, staring up at Kilgerrin. "What makes you say that?"

He grinned. "You forget I'm a wastrel who fills his days with social affairs, sporting events, and club life. In the course of all that, one hears things."

"What exactly have you heard?"

"I'd rather wait until there's some conclusive evidence, Alicia. Otherwise I'd simply be passing on gossip."

The girl sat up and moved slightly away from him. "Is it that you don't trust me to keep a secret?"

Reaching out, he caught both her hands in his. "For the moment, my dear, you have to trust me," he said. "Eventually I'll be able to . . . eventually you'll understand."

"I thought we were to have no secrets," she said. "There was to be nothing held back."

"Between us, no. There are some secrets, though, which aren't entirely mine."

"I don't quite understand."

"I simply can't explain further now."

"I see." She slipped her hands out of his, folded her arms, and retreated to the far side of the carriage cab.

The fog pressed at the small windows in the doors. They floated through late-night London almost soundlessly.

After a moment Kilgerrin asked, "You're not still consulting Dr. Marryat, are you?"

The girl stiffened, not immediately answering. "No," she said at last.

"I've heard some rather unpleasant things about him and—"

"My, you seem to have become a veritable sponge for gossip, Rob. Have you even soaked up some fascinating tidbits about me?"

"Alicia, I didn't intend to—"

"Why is it you're always so intent on quizzing me lately? I feel I'm a witness at the Old Bailey, or perhaps someone accused of a crime."

"Forgive me," he said. "My fondness for you has prompted me to be much too curious, I fear."

"You've done a good deal of speechifying about this fondness, Rob, and yet I—"

He moved, took her in his arms, kissed her.

There was no further conversation during the remainder of the drive to Darkside Court.

Chapter 11

"It's that sort of night, miss."

"What sort, Meggs?"

"The sort when ghosts walk and graves open," said the squat, round-shouldered housemaid while she turned down the blankets on Alicia's bed. "When the fog stalks the streets, miss, and there's a certain chilliness in the air, you may be sure summat will happen."

From her dressing table, where she was letting down her auburn hair, the girl said, "Tonight's been most pleasant thus far."

"How's that?" inquired the old woman, cupping a hand to her ear.

"I don't share your premonitions, Meggs," said Alicia in a louder voice. "Tonight has been quite pleasant so far."

"Ah, that's because Cupid's been using you for a dart board, miss," observed Meggs. "Well do I remember my own girlhood, long ago as it was, when I was courted by the likes of Ned Sparhawk. What a dashing figure did Ned cut, and when they hanged the darling boy, I fair wept for days on end, miss."

"You've never mentioned him before," said Alicia while she combed out her hair. "Hanged, was he?"

"Right outside of Newgate Prison, for all the world to see. Have you never heard of Dashin' Ned? In his day he was quite a notorious highwayman. Handsome he was, too, and strong as Samson. But for a small wen right about here on his dear face he was near as good looking, miss, as your own Mr. Kilgerrin. That he was, poor Ned." Her breath sighed out. "Long ago it all was. Shall I fetch you a bedwarmer?"

"That won't be necessary, Meggs."

"Then I'll be off, miss, and wishing you a pleasant good evening." The old woman went shuffling to the door. "I trust I haven't frightened you with all my ghost chatter."

"Not at all." Alicia crossed to her bed. "There's nothing more soothing than a good ghostly tale at bedtime. Good night now."

The squat housemaid departed, and Alicia, after extinguishing the lamp, climbed into bed. She lay on her back, hands locked behind her head.

The events of the evening paraded through her mind, disjointed and fragmented. A Miss Besant pounded at the piano, Rob took her in his strong arms, Lord Cranford glared at her, fog spun all around her, Rob kissed her, the cold eyes of Lord Cranford, the flickering piano keys . . .

. . . cold and she'd come out without anything over her shoulders. Late it was, the moon wrapped in tatters of black cloud. Alicia made her way along the curving path toward the stables. Up in her room she'd heard something, some small but out-of-the-ordinary sound. Probably it was nothing, yet she decided to come down to the stables to make certain nothing was wrong.

The clouds thickened around the moon, the darkness increased, and she could hardly see. She knew her way to the stables by heart—there wasn't a square inch of Ravenshaw Court she wasn't thoroughly familiar with.

Figures behind that building there, near the back of the stall where her favorite mount was kept. In a brief flash of moonlight she could make out three men.

One of them was her Uncle Tobias. The others seemed very familiar, but she couldn't make out exactly who they were.

Uncle Tobias held a pistol.

He was pointing it directly at one of the shadowy figures.

He was going to fire.

Alicia must prevent it.

"Don't shoot!" she cried, running toward them. "Uncle Toby, for the love of God, don't shoot him!"

She kept running, stumbling, falling. She cried out.

"Don't shoot him! Uncle Toby, don't kill him!"

But the gun flashed and then . . .

"Child, child, whatever is wrong?"

The gaunt white face of Queen Bess was floating over her in the darkness.

Alicia blinked and struggled to breathe. She

found it very difficult to get air into her lungs and then sit up. A weight seemed to be pressing down on her chest.

"You've been screaming like someone possessed of a demon, child."

Finally she could sit up and the air came rushing into her. "Another dream, I'm afraid, Aunt," she said. "Forgive me."

Her aunt took hold of her wrist. "You were crying out the most fantastic things, dear," she said. "Do you remember?"

Swallowing, the girl shook her head. "No, nothing," she answered, not quite truthfully. "What was I saying?"

"Oh, I don't wish to repeat any of it." Aunt Elizabeth's head drifted nearer to the girl's. "Can you remember nothing of your nightmare?"

"I can't, no." She'd been perspiring, her nightdress was clinging damply to her breasts. "Why do you ask?"

"It occurred to me that if we knew the matter of these horrible dreams, we might be better able to deal with them."

"I'm afraid it all shattered like a dropped wine goblet when I awakened. I try to recall the details, but I can't put it back together again."

The old woman nodded slowly. "Would you like me to sit up with you a bit, Alicia?"

"That won't be necessary, Queen Bess. Usually, you know, I don't suffer more than one of—"

Something thumped onto the bed, landing between the girl's legs. A small furious growling commenced.

"Dante, stop that at once," warned Aunt Eliza-

68

beth. "You're not allowed on Alicia's bed, and most certainly you're not to nibble at the quilt."

The little dog had his teeth sunk into the quilt and was shaking his stubby head from side to side as though shaking the life out of some prey.

"Perhaps you ought to let him remain, Aunt, to scare away any stray goblins."

"This is not a matter for jesting over." The old woman dealt the dog a slap on the backside. "Enough, you naughty creature. These nightmares of yours are serious, very serious. Dante, you little bounder, cease!"

Dante continued to chew at the blankets, growling ominously in his tiny chest.

Aunt Elizabeth finally resorted to yanking him up by his collar, then prying the quilt from between his teeth. "You're a very bad fellow."

Straightening the blankets, Alicia rested her head on her pillow. "I'm sorry I awakened the both of you," she said. "I do believe I'll be able to get through the rest of the night with no further trouble."

Tucking the subsiding Dante up under her arm, Aunt Elizabeth asked, "Are you certain, child, you remember nothing of what you were dreaming about?"

"Not a bit of it."

"Good night, then. Hush, Dante." She left the bedchamber, shutting the door quietly after her.

"I do remember," Alicia said to herself. "But not enough, not yet."

Chapter 12

It was one of the most fashionable residences in the very fashionable Earl's Terrace. On the outside, at any rate.

Inside, Lord MacQuarrie's home was a testament to the pitfalls of bachelor life. For one thing, nothing ever managed to return to its proper place. Thus a pair of Hessian boots and a coal scuttle shared the wing chair in the library into which Lord MacQuarrie's one-eyed butler led Rob Kilgerrin. And on the drop-front desk, along with a confusion of papers and notes, sat an unstrung violin.

"I do hope you'll forgive the disarray hereabouts, sir," said Eames, his single green eye watching Kilgerrin hopefully. "Mrs. Eames and I does the best we can, but he always manages to keep well in advance of our efforts. On top of which, I don't imagine you'll mind my alluding to, he keeps us continually hopping, as it were, in areas which have little or nothing to do, to my way of thinking at least, with keeping up a spic and span household. Last evening, to take but one example from a multitude, he sent me clear to Lambeth to deliver a most urgent missive. Betimes he had my dear wife fixing up a well-laden picnic hamper for a group of chaps who was off to Brighton at a most unusual hour."

"I quite understand." Grinning, Kilgerrin removed a handful of unsmoked cigars from the cane-bottom chair near Lord Mac's desk and seated himself.

"Not, mind you, that I intend to complain," continued Eames. "This is by far the most pleasant situation myself and my dear wife have ever had the good fortune to possess. And, you may take my word for it, there's never a bit of boredom here with Lord Mac. When I served the late Colonel Hartwell, who got the unfortunate notion Turkish secret agents were surrounding his quaint old mansion in Barchester, the old gentleman couldn't be made to leave his bed for weeks on end. The result was, sir, that life with the colonel was somewhat sort of invigorating."

"Yes, I can well imagine life around Lord Mac would be one thing after the other."

"Well put, sir, most well put." Avoiding a beaver hat which was on the floor, Eames made his way to the doorway. "I'd best fetch him, hadn't I?" He left with a bobbing bow of his head.

A cloud of smoke preceded Lord MacQuarrie into the room a few moments later. "I wasn't expecting you, Rob."

Kilgerrin stood. "Several matters have arisen."

71

"Pertaining to Alicia Kingsley?" MacQuarrie flicked ashes in the general direction of a vase.

"I'm having, Lord Mac, a very difficult time resolving the difficulties this assignment has created."

"Yes, I'm aware of that."

"It might be better if I shifted to some other—"

"A shift, Rob, might well mean you wouldn't be able to see the girl at all."

Kilgerrin's fists clenched involuntarily. "No, I can't have that," he said firmly. "You see, I've . . . fallen in love with Alicia. I can't stay away from her, and yet I feel dishonest in not being able to confide in her what my original purpose is."

"You cannot do that," cautioned Lord Mac-Quarrie, spewing out smoke. "Your job is to expose those who are collaborating with the agents of Bonaparte. Confiding in anyone, no matter how close you are and how much you may trust her, will jeopardize your work."

"I haven't forgotten." Kilgerrin ran a hand through his dark hair. "Being less than truthful with her is wearing me down."

MacQuarrie sat on a cane-bottom chair, after moving aside three volumes of the essays of Hazlitt. "Being in love with the girl is, I admit, a complication," he acknowledged. "Have you considered, though, the very strong possibility she herself may well be in danger?"

"Is that a conjecture or a fact?"

"After you passed on to me the fragments of information your gross and drunken friend, Rowdybranch, gave you, I—"

"He's a very honest and a very gifted man."

"Well, I never feel quite comfortable around satirists," MacQuarrie admitted. "I grant you the man has talent as an artist, even though his recent depiction of me in the guise of an ass was not, to my way of thinking, in the best of taste." He puffed on his cigar. "Didn't look that much like me, either, yet several of my friends chided me that it was a striking portrait. Be that as it may, Rob. There does seem to be a link between this Dr. Marryat and Lord Cranford. By putting a watch on Marryat we've learned he does on occasion communicate with our illustrious cabinet minister. Something we should have been aware of long since."

"We've always considered Cranford a man above reproach."

"We'll apparently have to reappraise him."

"You feel the danger to Alicia will come from him, Lord Mac?"

"While Lord Cranford has had a reputation for loyalty, he has never been noted for his warmth," replied MacQuarrie. "I do believe that if Alicia Kingsley stands in his way, he won't hesitate to sweep her aside."

"I can't see her as a threat to him, even if the man is on Bonaparte's side and not ours."

"He now knows you and the young lady are quite close. He is also aware of your true calling, Rob." The older man blew out a stream of smoke. "We can keep a close watch on Cranford," he said. "As yet, though, we have little or nothing in the way of proof. Far from enough to persuade anyone to take action against a man of his public reputation, not even in wartime."

Rob began pacing the room. "I have, as deftly as I can, tried to find out whatever Alicia might know about the activities of her uncle," he said. "I'll swear she knows nothing."

"Or at least thinks she knows nothing."

He halted, staring. "What do you mean by that?"

"You're forgetting Dr. Marryat's speciality," said Lord MacQuarrie.

Chapter 13

Tobias Copplestone remembered where he'd placed his tobacco jar. He located it and stuffed tobacco into the bowl of his clay pipe with a chubby forefinger. Lighting the mixture, he settled his substantial bulk into a fat armchair and stretched his legs out until his slippered feet were quite comfortably close to the grate of the fireplace in his study. A cheery blaze was crackling away, its glowing warmth compensating for the sharp wind that was worrying at the stained glass windows of this oak-paneled room. The branches of the surrounding elms ticked at the tinted squares of glass.

Copplestone was a man in his late fifties, plump and red of face. After a few puffs on his pipe, he reached over to the low table beside him to pick up his paper knife and the first volume of the newest novel sent down from London. He'd just finished a long and unsettling session with the manager of the Ravenshaw estate, and his main wish now was to read himself into a better time and place and then doze away what was left of the afternoon.

Although he believed fervently in the cause he secretly served, Alicia's uncle was not an overly zealous man. He believed in working when work had to be done, then in resting as comfortably as was possible until the next challenge presented itself.

He settled deeper into his chair, turned to the first chapter of the novel. Judging by the abundance of witches, bravos, and squint-eyed gypsies in the frontispiece engraving, the book would be a good one.

There was a sudden knocking on the thick oaken door of his study. Or rather, there were two series of knocks, the first polite and timid, the second bold and impatient.

"Yes, what is it?" Copplestone set the novel aside and grumbled up out of his snug chair.

The door swung a few inches open. "Begging your pardon, sir, but this fellow insists on—"

"Enough folderol," put in a deep, slightly blurred voice. "I'll state me business direct to the squire."

"Tanner!" exclaimed Copplestone, considerably surprised to see who the intruder was. "Is there something amiss at Darkside Square?"

"Would I submit me posterior to the foul punishment of a saddle if all was sweetness and light, now?" The butler from London came into the room. A huge man, ill-shaven, clad all in black.

"I'll attend to this, Miller." Copplestone made a

shooing gesture at his own frail servitor and the door was shut from the outside.

"Is there nothing to drink in this establishment?" Tanner demanded as he glanced around the paneled room.

"You'll find decanters on the sideboard yonder," said Copplestone. "Help yourself to whatever you think you require, then tell me what brings you here, for pity's sake."

The broad-backed Tanner was busy tugging out cut-glass stoppers and sniffing at the contents of the half-dozen decanters which decorated the top of the richly carved sideboard. "No rum?"

Copplestone's nose wrinkled. "Certainly not. Now, man, do explain yourself!"

"No need of that, since I've brung you a billet doux from 'er 'ighness." After a few more questioning sniffs, he decided on brandy and poured himself a hefty portion.

"Well, where is it?"

Very slowly and enthusiastically, Tanner drained the contents of his glass. He wiped his lips on his sleeve. "Weak stuff that, squire," he observed. "Now then, to business, as it were." He started his rough hands moving over himself, patting and searching. "Got the bloody note right 'ere summers."

"By Jove, Tanner, you're the most exasperating messenger it's ever been my—"

"Calm yourself, squire, 'ere it is, for a fact." He tugged a folded note out of an inner pocket, lurched slightly to the right, and handed it over to Tobias Copplestone. "From good Queen Bess 'erself it is." Turning his back on his host, he gave his attention once more to the array of decanters.

Stubby fingers quivering slightly, Copplestone broke the scarlet wax seal and unfolded the note. The message was brief and in Elizabeth's unmistakable scrawl.

It said: I fear she is starting to *remember!* You must take action very *quickly.*

Alicia's uncle read the message twice more before moving to the fireplace and consigning it to the flames.

A moment he'd long dreaded had finally arrived.

Chapter 14

The eyes glowed. They caught the firelight, seemed to send it flashing across the room at Tobias Copplestone.

"By Jove, Marryat, I wish you wouldn't use that gimlet gaze on me," he protested. "I'm not one of your confounded subjects." Attempting to move out of the range of the wizened doctor's stare, Alicia's uncle bumped into the dangling skeleton.

"Will you, Tobias, settle down in one spot." Dr. Marryat was hunched down in a large wing chair.

"Can't see, for the life of me, why you insist on displaying such a thing." Copplestone sat down, uneasily. "You've nothing much to do with a chap's bones after all."

"It merely serves as a momento mori, Tobias," replied the little doctor, reaching into a pocket of his spattered waistcoat. "Now, pray, explain to me the cause of your sudden rush to our great city."

"I have spent, Marryat, a very unpleasant afternoon with my Aunt Elizabeth." Copplestone placed his palms on his broad knees. "Yes, very unpleasant."

"Since any time passed in the company of that harridan is by definition unpleasant," observed Dr. Marryat as he slid his ivory-lidded snuffbox out, "I have yet to hear anything surprising or unusual, Tobias."

"Elizabeth informs me she's already consulted you about the condition of my niece."

"Ah." Dr. Marryat paused in the midst of delivering a pinch of snuff to a nostril. "We come to the heart of the matter."

"Confound it, Marryat, the child's starting to remember." Copplestone stood, sat again. "We can't, I needn't mention, have that."

"Were you and your dear aunt somewhat less sentimental, Tobias, the simplest solution to this little problem would long ago have been carried out." He thrust the snuff into his nose.

Copplestone rose to his feet, this time staying on them. "That's a monstrous suggestion," he said in an angry voice. "The girl is not to be harmed."

"The girl is not to be harmed," mocked the little doctor before giving out a resounding sneeze. "Instead we're all to hang on the gibbet."

Moving closer to the sniffling doctor, Alicia's uncle pointed at him. "If you'd done your job as you boasted you could, Marryat, we'd none of us have a thing to worry about now."

"There is always a slight possibility of something going wrong." The doctor shut his snuffbox. "I assure you I am the most accomplished mesmerist in England, Tobias, and no one else could have done a more thorough job of erasing certain unpleasant facts from that foolish girl's mind." He stood to face the other. "Yet there are times, albeit rare, when something goes awry."

"She wasn't supposed to remember, wasn't to recall a single event of that dreadful evening," said Copplestone accusingly. "Instead we find she's crying out in her sleep, all sorts of frightful accusations."

"Thus far, let me remind you, all recollections of what actually occurred at Ravenshaw Court fade from her mind upon awakening."

"Thus far, granted," said Copplestone. "Can you guarantee, doctor, that some fine morning soon Alicia will not retain a clear picture of everything her troubled dreams seem so intent on telling her?"

Shaking his head, Dr. Marryat answered, "Unfortunately, I can not."

"We must, therefore, take steps."

Absently brushing specks of snuff from the front of himself, the little doctor moved to the fireplace and stood staring at the blaze. "You must take the girl to Ravenshaw as soon as possible," he said. "I'll journey there once I attend to certain affairs here in London."

Copplestone frowned. "The girl, partly because of certain suggestions you yourself implanted, has little fondness these days for Ravenshaw Court."

"You're not to give her any choice in the matter. You are simply to see Alicia is there when I arrive two days hence," Marryat told him. "I require complete privacy and solitude to work again on the girl's mind. London is out of the question if I am to bury for good and all what she knows."

"I'll attend to it, then." Copplestone moved toward the door, retrieving his beaver hat. "We can definitely expect you at Ravenshaw in two days then?"

"Yes, and see you have the girl there when I arrive."

"You're certain you can remedy this?"

"Yes, of course."

Nodding, Copplestone placed his hat on his head and took his leave, a look of deep concern on his plump face.

When the visitor was gone, the little doctor crossed to the dangling skeleton and stroked the top of its glazed skull. "Oh, yes," he muttered, "I'll remedy things. One way or another."

Rain and darkness arrived together. The rain was heavy, slanting down through the new blackness. It clattered on the fanlight over Dr. Marryat's door, pattered on the roof of the carriage which drew up to his door as the bells in nearby St. Norbert's Church tolled eight.

The doctor's front door creaked open as the last stroke of the hour faded away in the rainy night. Old Marryat himself, muffled in a dark greatcoat, came hurrying out of the house. The shadow from the brim of his hat served to mask his penetrating little eyes. But within that band of shadow the eyes were watchful. Satisfying himself there were no hostile observers about, the doctor stepped quickly across the pavement and into the carriage. He gave the address of Lord Cranford, and the carriage went clattering away into the rain and darkness.

From an alley across the cobblestoned street a dark figure emerged—a figure Dr. Marryat's careful scrutiny had failed to detect. A man, but whether young or old, lean or stout, the thick black cloak most thoroughly hid. The watcher, his vigil ended for the time being, went hurrying away in a direction opposite to that just taken by the departing doctor.

Chapter 15

Alicia stirred, moaned, and then sat up awake. "What is it?"

Chill fingers touched her bare shoulder.

Her aunt, fully dressed, stood beside the girl's bed. "We must leave at once, child," she informed her.

"Leave?" Alicia rubbed her eyes. "For where, Queen Bess?"

"Your uncle needs us at Ravenshaw."

The girl shivered. "But Uncle Toby was here only yesterday, and he made no mention of—"

"Circumstances," Aunt Elizabeth informed her, "have changed rather suddenly."

Almost mechanically, Alicia slid out of her warm bed. She allowed her aunt to help her into her dressing gown. "Is Uncle Toby ill? He appeared to be in excellent health."

"Your uncle is no worse than usual," said the old woman impatiently. "Something has arisen which requires us all to be at Ravenshaw Court most urgently."

"I . . . never seem to enjoy myself there any longer." Alicia went to the window. The early morning outside was thick with fog. "Is it absolutely necessary I go?"

"According to your uncle, it most certainly is," said Aunt Elizabeth. "Now, child, do get yourself ready to travel. We must leave within a very few hours, and there's much to be attended to before I can safely leave this house in the hands of two such as Meggs and Tanner."

Frowning, the girl asked, "How long shall we be staying there, Aunt Elizabeth?"

"No longer than is necessary, child."

"Can you translate that into days?"

"I imagine we shan't be away from London for more than a month."

"A month." This unexpected and apparently extended absense from the city didn't at all fit into such plans as she'd been making, plans for herself and the handsome Rob Kilgerrin. Besides, she always felt so uneasy when she was at her old home. "I won't be going," she announced.

The old woman came striding across the room to take hold of her bare arm. "You will, child. There's no debating about it. Your uncle has summoned us, and go we must."

"But I had intended to—"

"If it's that young Kilgerrin who's causing you to fret, write him a note."

"I'd much prefer to remain in London."

Her aunt's grip on her arm tightened. "Out of the question, child."

Alicia hesitated, then gave in. "Very well, I'll go," she said. "But I will write a letter to Mr. Kilgerrin and leave it here for him. He was planning to call this very aft—"

"Yes, yes, by all means." Aunt Elizabeth let go of the girl and headed for the doorway. "Make it brief, Alicia, we haven't a good deal of time to waste."

After her aunt departed, the girl remained at the window watching the swirling fog.

"Nothing?"

"Exactly, sir," confirmed Tanner, swaying slightly on the threshold. "Not a blinkin' word, sir, not a snippet of farewell."

"Then apparently they left in somewhat of a hurry," said Kilgerrin, standing on the brick front steps of the Darkside Square house.

There had of course been a letter, quite a lengthy and tender one, left behind by Alicia. Tanner had, at the express instruction of Aunt Elizabeth, long since burned it in the drawing room fireplace.

"That they did," agreed the butler. "Was there anything else, sir?"

"Yes, Tanner, I'd like very much to know where Miss Kingsley went."

"On that count I am unable to assist you," he replied. "I know only that Miss Kingsley and 'er aunt departed in summat of a rush. It is my notion they do not intend to return to London for a matter of some weeks."

"Some weeks." Kilgerrin stroked his chin. "Can I conclude that they've gone to Ravenshaw?"

"Anything is possible, sir, in a world so full of possibilities." Tanner wiped at his perspiring brow. "They may 'ave gone to Ravenshaw Court, and they may not 'ave. I am able to tell you nothing more."

"Oh, I'm certain you could if I were to take the time to persuade you," said Kilgerrin, with a smile which was far from cordial. "For the moment, however, I'll merely wish you good afternoon."

"And the same to you, sir, I'm sure."

Out on the street Kilgerrin stood gazing back at Alicia's house for several moments. He was not at all pleased with the turn of events, believing the girl would not have left London willingly without communicating with him in some way.

"Unless someone prevented her," he thought.

The most sensible course of action seemed to be to travel to Ravenshaw and determine if Alicia were indeed there. If she were, though, and nothing appeared to be wrong, he might have some difficulty explaining why he'd come all the way from London.

"Damn it, I'm in love with her, after all," he reminded himself. "I don't need an excuse for following her to Ravenshaw ... or to the ends of the Earth, for that matter."

Yes, that's what he'd do. He'd make the necessary arrangements and be under way in less than an hour.

Chapter 16

The mingled scents, engraver's acid and raw rum, told him who was awaiting him in his drawing room.

"Thomas," said Kilgerrin with a pleased grin. "What brings you here?"

Thumping his cudgel into the carpet, Rowdybranch levered himself to a standing position. His gouty foot had an extra swathing of bandages around it this afternoon. "Only the most serious emergency, by Hecate, could pull me forth from the dubious comforts of my little snuggery over the redoubtable Mrs. Draper's place of business."

Kilgerrin said, "I'm about to depart for—"

"You'll have to cancel any plans, Rob," the massive artist informed him. "There's need of you at Ravenshaw Court."

Kilgerrin's eyes widened. "Why, Thomas, that's exactly where I'm bound. Tell me, what do you know of all this?"

Pinching at his bulb of a nose, Rowdybranch replied, "Alicia is in danger."

Kilgerrin gripped his friend's fat arm. "Do they mean to kill her?"

"Not yet, my boy. But they intend to place her once again in the hands of that quacksalver, Marryat," said Rowdybranch. "I know there are others, most particularly the eagle-beaked Lord Cranford, who'd like to do much worse."

Kilgerrin bit his knuckle. "How did you learn of this?"

"Have I not already told you I am the best-informed man in all of London? Since our last confabulation I've increased my scrutiny of the rogues who're interested in your young lady. Thus it is I know her conniving uncle rushed up to town two days since and, after an anxious interview with his superannuated aunt, hied himself to the offices of the good Dr. Marryat. After which consultation, Marryat paid a visit on none other than Lord Cranford."

"You think Cranford ordered Alicia taken out of London?"

"I think he may even have ordered her death."

"But why? I don't—"

"The girl quite obviously must know something they don't want known. The minstrations of Marryat have not, so I would judge, succeeded in suppressing the incriminating facts or erasing them from the young lady's mind," explained the massive artist. "It is my conclusion that Tobias Copplestone believes he'll convey Alicia to Ravenshaw Court where that quack can have another go at expunging whatever secret it is she holds within her pretty skull. Lord Cranford, my boy, is not a man noted for his patience. He may move to destroy the girl once she reaches Ravenshaw . . . or even while she is en route."

Kilgerrin said, "She may have left hours ago."

"Nevertheless, you must try to catch up with her," advised Rowdybranch. "Then you must persuade her to return to London."

"I'll leave at once." He spun on his heel and ran for the doorway.

"You must ride like the proverbial wind," Rowdybranch called after him.

Chapter 17

Dusk caught up with them in forest country.
Oaks and elms stretched away on each side of the
roadway. The last of the daylight was drifting away,
velvety dark was starting to fill in the spaces between the uneven rows of trees.

Dante, suffering a troubled sleep, made a mournful growling noise from his position on Aunt Elizabeth's narrow lap.

"Hush, hush," she murmured, patting his furrowed forehead.

This stretch of road was rich with dust, and it
billowed up as their carriage rolled, bumping and
swaying, toward Ravenshaw Court.

"Hadn't we ought to consider," ventured Alicia,
"stopping for the night?"

"Nonsense," responded Queen Bess. "The inns in this part of the country are little better than sties. Besides which, child, we are certain to reach Ravenshaw in less than two hours, even relying on these feeble horses your dear uncle has seen fit to provide for us. You can surely put up with a bit more discomfort."

"It's not the discomfort, Aunt," said the girl. "I'm thinking more of our safety."

"I've traveled over these very roads most of my life, traveled them when they were mere cowpaths, and I have yet . . ."

With much snorting and tromping on the part of the horses, their carriage abruptly came to a halt on the twilight road.

Dante unexpectedly lost his position on the old woman's knees and went sailing into the empty seat opposite. He commenced yelping in protest.

"Silence, you naughty beast." Pushing the whimpering dog aside, Aunt Elizabeth leaned and opened the door on her side of the carriage a few inches. "What in heaven's name is the cause of this unwarranted and—"

A pistol went off. Up on the box their driver moaned once, then fell over with a resounding thud.

"Aunt Liz, what's happening out there?" Alicia, one hand pressed to her throat moved to the other door.

The darkness outside grew suddenly blacker. She realized a cloaked and muffled figure had moved to stand immediately in front of the door.

"What are you blackguards up to?" Aunt Elizabeth was crying out. "Have you any idea of who we are? I warn you Tobias Copplestone is a power hereabouts. When he is made aware of this outrage—"

"Shut your mouth, you old harpy," advised a gruff voice out in the darkness.

The old woman gasped. "I know that voice," she murmured. Flinging her door wide, she began struggling to get out. "You there, I know who you are, and I am fully aware of who sent you."

"You'd best keep that to yourself, nanny."

"You'll not do this! The plan calls for something entirely—" Realizing Alicia was listening to her, Aunt Elizabeth ceased speaking and stood on the dusty road gazing at the three horsemen who ringed the front of their traveling carriage.

Alicia tentatively opened her door. The warm night wind carried to her all at once the smells of the figure who waited out there. A rough blend of rum and barnyard.

"Come on out, won't yer, missy," invited a raspy voice. "Save me ther trouble o' fetchin' yer, won't it now."

"We have very little money, no jewelry at all," she told him, fighting to keep herself from shivering. She remained in the carriage doorway, one foot dangling out into the night.

"'Urry it up, missy. We ain't got all the blessed evenin' ter spen' on this yere business now, 'ave we." A rough hairy hand came reaching for her.

The dormant Dante decided to take action. Growling fiercely, he leaped right at the man who was making a grab for Alicia.

His aim was accurate, his sharp tiny teeth sank into the man's fingers.

"Fire and damnation! What in the bloody 'ell's

got 'old er me now?" He took a few steps back, swatting at the dog that clung to his bleeding hand.

Alicia kicked out at him, her foot connecting with his chest.

He gave a surprised roar, staggered, and toppled down onto his backside. Dante let go his hand and made a try for the stubbly face.

The girl jumped free of the carriage and started to run.

"What's going on over there?" cried one of the other men.

"Hugh's letting her get away!"

There was no time for anything except running. Wrapping her traveling cloak tightly around her, Alicia fled into the surrounding woods. To her ears she was making an incredible amount of noise as she stumbled and staggered over dead leaves and fallen twigs. Thorns tore at her clothes and at her flesh, twisted branches whipped at her, unseen forest creatures went scuttling and scurrying out of her way.

"Over 'ere! She's 'eadin' that there way!"

" 'Ell with 'er. Get this bloomin' monster orf me afore 'e minches me features."

"After her! We can't let her escape alive!"

They really meant to kill her, then. Alicia had no idea why, she only knew she must keep running. Must get away from them.

She didn't even know what they looked like; they were only dark shapes briefly seen. Even the man who'd tried to drag her from the carriage she'd got only a fleeting glimpse of.

Something was rattling, drawing attention to her.

Alicia realized it was the coin pouch she carried in an inner pocket of her cloak. Running, tripping, bumping against tree trunks, tangling with twists of brush, she still managed to get a hand into the pocket. She snatched out the pouch and held it tightly clenched in one fist, killing the jingle.

"I 'ear 'er! Over this way!"

"That's only Will tramping around."

"It ain't, I tell yer!"

The voices seemed no closer, and the darkness was richer and thicker in here. Alicia slowed, concentrating on moving as quietly as she—

An unsuspected snarl of tree root underfoot and she went sprawling. The coin purse flew from her grasp to go rattling to a landing off in a patch of nettles.

Did they hear that?

"This way! Come on, Will!"

No, they were moving in a different direction, voices getting fainter.

On her hands and knees, breath grating into her lungs, she debated about the coins. Ought she to abandon the pouch or waste time searching for it here in the thorny dark?

She might well need money, alone as she was, not even certain where she was.

Crawling forward, she began to poke at the thorny brush. The sharp branches ripped at the skin of her hands, scraped and poked. Finally, it seemed long moments later, she heard a jingling. Her bleeding fingers closed over the money pouch and she stood up.

After drawing in a deep breath, she started moving again. As quietly as she could, Alicia headed in the one direction she felt might be safe. That was away from their carriage and the road they'd been traveling.

Despite all the confusion and anxiety, the fear and the running, she remembered very clearly what her aunt had said to the highwaymen.

Aunt Elizabeth had made it very obvious she recognized at least one of the men who'd stopped them and shot their driver. The old woman had told them, "You're not following the plan, it's supposed to be done differently."

It seemed so incredible, yet what else could she believe? Somehow, for reasons completely mysterious to her, someone wished to kill her. Yes, the attackers had alluded to that several times. Their objective was to murder her.

And her aunt was somehow involved in it. Aunt Elizabeth, and it must be Uncle Toby as well, both had some reason for wishing her dead.

The sudden uprooting, the hurried journey toward Ravenshaw Court, all of it tied in. Tied in with some plan to murder her.

"Incredible," the girl whispered as she made her way through the night woods.

There was, then, no safe place for her. Should she go to Ravenshaw, she'd put herself directly at the mercy of the two people she was now convinced desired her death. The house in Darkside Square was equally unsafe, since if she appeared there, Tanner would alert her aunt and uncle at once.

"Rob," she realized.

Yes, there remained one place of sanctuary. That was with Rob Kilgerrin.

He was in London, though, a good sixty miles away.

Nevertheless, no matter how long it might take, and even if she must travel the long, weary way on foot, Alicia made up her mind she must get to Rob.

With him, with his strong arms around her, she felt she would be safe from any threat.

She kept moving, stumbling, falling, rising. She struggled through the thick forest, listening for some sound of pursuit.

There was nothing. Only the night sounds of the woodland.

Even so, she couldn't risk stopping to rest.

She must keep on.

Chapter 18

Through the trees she saw light, very small squares of light floating in the darkness a long way off. Alicia paused, wiping the back of her hand over her cheek. Her auburn hair hung in uneven curls across her perspiring forehead. She was dusty and tattered, and there were thin smears of blood on her hands and arms.

Though slim, she was sturdy, and she knew she could continue on until she reached those distant lights.

"I pray they're friendly."

Alicia started on her way once more, her pace a bit slower, her gait not quite so confident. She'd been struggling through the forest for hours now. She wasn't certain exactly how long.

She had lost her pursuers, of that she was certain. This was no time to relax and let down her guard, however. She was a long way from London and Rob Kilgerrin and the security and safety he represented.

"I still don't understand," she said to herself. It was evident Aunt Elizabeth and Uncle Tobias wanted her dead. But why? Could the reason be the land and money she was to fall heir to when she reached the age of twenty-five? That was ridiculous; her relatives couldn't be behaving like the incredible characters in a melodrama. There must be some other reason.

"The dreams," Alicia said aloud. "The reason must be the dreams I've been having. Yes, they realize the dreams will . . ."

She'd almost caught hold of it. Something inside her mind that would provide an answer. She couldn't hold on to it, try as she might.

"There's something I must remember."

But what?

The sound of heavy hoofbeats cut across her speculations. The girl stopped still and pressed herself against the broad bole of an oak.

She was near a road at last. As she stood, waiting and watching, two horsemen went galloping by not more than a hundred yards from her.

Alicia remained where she was until the riders were gone, then started moving once again. There were buildings across the road, less than a quartermile away now. Two large buildings and a cluster of smaller ones. Their windows glowed a warm yellow.

This must be an inn. There'd be people there and, at least temporarily, safety.

The sign hung on a rod of twisted iron, creaking in the gentle night wind.

Alicia frowned up, made out the words The Martyr's Head and a faded portrait of a bloody severed head.

The inn buildings circled an unevenly paved courtyard and looked, in the dim light spilling out from within, like an impossibly tilting collection of steeply slanting shingle roofs, vastly lopsided brick chimneys, off-kilter leaded windows, and much ancient whitewashed rock and dark crossbeams. Boldly lettered on the whitewashed wall near the main door was Ales & Stout and Hogg, Prop.

A horse nickered in the stables across the bumpy flagstones, and Alicia started.

"Lor, miss, whatever in the great world happened to you?"

She turned and saw a tall thin boy of about fourteen watching her from an arched doorway a few feet off. He was smoking the battered remains of a cigar and had his hands hidden under the long apron he wore. The apron nearly touched the ground and was much spotted.

"An accident," said Alicia. "My carriage was . . . attacked by highwaymen."

"Bless me, I sincerely hopes they done you no serious harm."

She shook her head, aware of the sorry state of her hair. "No . . . I was able to get away."

"Was there any killin'? I mean to say, was the rest of your party ruthlessly slaughtered?"

"I don't believe so," she replied. "Now can you tell me where I can arrange to be taken back to London?"

"Right here on this very spot, miss." The boy

discarded his fragment of cigar and approached nearer.

"Thank goodness. When?"

"It'll be the Flying Eagle coach you'll be wantin'," the boy explained. "Goes from here to London in no more than six hours if all conditions are favorable."

"Yes, but when does it leave?"

"Bright and early tomorrow," the kitchen boy told her.

Alicia sighed. "There's no way I can leave for London before then?"

"'Fraid not, miss," the boy said. "Is it some dire peril you're in and some urgent—"

"Davey! You wastrel, where've you gotten to?" called a voice from inside.

"I'd best be returnin' to my chores, miss." The boy glanced furtively around. "If you does stay here the night, watch out for—"

"Aha, Davey! So it's here I find you, you lazy scoundrel, reeking of that devilish weed and . . . Ah, but good evening, miss. What may I do to serve you?" The innkeep relaxed the grip he'd affected on Davey's soiled collar when he'd come charging out into the courtyard. A crooked smile played on his lips. Bowing, he said in a more polite voice, "I am Sebastian Hogg himself, the noted owner and proprietor of the famed Martyr's Head, an inn believed to have been built during the reign of Richard II and kept in an excellent and heartwarming state of repair ever since by untold illustrious generations of Hoggs. Why, only last week a noted London periodical saw fit to—"

"She was attacked by brigands," interrupted Davey while he twisted out of the innkeeper's grip.

"Murdered all her friends and relatives by a-slittin' their throats and—"

"Back to the kitchen, you mooncalf," suggested Hogg, giving the boy a helpful prod with his elbow.

"What I mean to say is, she don't want no legend and lore, sir, what she stands in need of is—"

"Begone, ungrateful whelp, or I'll send you packing back to the Wordwood Orphanage before dawn breaks."

Davey, after giving the girl a warning frown, hurried back through the side door.

Bowing more solemnly, causing the buttons on his flowered waistcoat to strain, Hogg said, "You were indeed, forgive my rude curiosity, miss, actually assaulted by knights of the road? I'm most sorely distressed to hear such unhappy news, since the countryside around Cockleburr has been quite free of such annoyances for near to—"

"Is that where I am? Cockleburr?"

"Aye, miss, this is the pleasant, oft described as idyllic, village of Cockleburr. Noted far and wide as the birthplace, in the eventful year of 1686, of the noted poet, Ronald Hogg, who penned "To His Flirtatious Mistress's Shoe" and many another lyric of reknown. No relation, I must ruefully admit. It was in Cockleburr also that General Hopjoy had the brief and ill-fated interlude with the unfortunate Miss Jarvis," continued Hogg, commencing to breathe a little irregularly. "Cockleburr is also known, in song and story, as the site of the justly famous inn before which you—"

"I wonder if I might have lodging for the night?" The girl pulled her tattered cloak tighter around her slim body.

"Indeed you may, miss," said Hogg with a jovial chuckle. "One of the reasons the Martyr's Head is loved and respected throughout the length and breadth of Albion is for its gracious and near overwhelming hospitality." He paused, coughed into one hefty fist, and eyed her from beneath his thick eyebrows. "I trust those odious brigands didn't leave you without a penny?"

The girl opened her scratched hand to show him the pouch of coins. "I can pay for my room," she assured him. "As well as the coach fare back to London."

"Ah, so it's to London you wish to journey?" Eyes on the coins which could be observed bulging inside the chamois, he executed another bow. "The Flying Eagle will carry you thence like some swift winged creature of fable."

"But not until tomorrow morning?"

"Such is the case." Hogg waddled around her to the main doorway to his inn. "However, you shall find within these sacred portals the most elegant accommodations in all Christendom. Why, kings and princes have slept upon our goosedown and raved with enthusiastic praise. Indeed, when the late Bishop Anmar breathed his last while on a visit to the venerable city of Florence, he's rumored to have said, with his dying breath mind you, 'What a great pity I must die here and not in one of Hogg's splendid beds.' I cannot swear to the truth of the statement, miss, though you must admit it sounds plausible. Now let me invite you inside, and you can see for yourself the luxury that is synonymous with the name of Hogg." He opened the oaken door with an expansive sweep of his hand.

Alicia followed him inside to brightness and warmth.

Chapter 19

They came a few minutes beyond midnight.

Two horsemen, the hooves of their mounts clattering on the flagstones of the courtyard. The much-ridden horses snorted and pawed as one of the night riders dismounted and hurried to the door of the inn.

When he found the thick door locked, he began to thump on it with a gloved fist.

Alicia was aware of none of this. Exhausted from her long trek through the forest, she slept a deep and dreamless sleep in a cozy room on the other side of the Martyr's Head.

"Come now, someone must be alive in there!" The cloaked figure continued pounding on the door.

After another moment a flickering blob of light

could be seen through the inn's darkened windows.

A moment more, and the door was unbolted. "Ah, such eagerness the far-flung fame of the Martyr inspires," said Hogg as he swung his front door open wide. "Wayfarers will even attempt to break in, so anxious are they to lodge here." He was still fully clad, held a squat, wax-encrusted candle holder and candle at a level with his broad face. "Come in, sir. The Martyr's Head stands ready, no matter how late and unreasonable the hour, to serve any and—"

"You can best serve me, old man, by quickly telling me what I want to know."

Hogg took a backward step. "Old, is it? Why I was but forty-six on my last birthday, sir. Perhaps this dim light creates the illusion of—"

"We're looking for someone." The visitor took hold of the front of the innkeeper's flowered waistcoat.

"Maybe you ought ter rough 'im up a bit," suggested the other man, still in his saddle. "Punch 'is fat face some."

"There'll be no need for that," said the man who held fast to the innkeeper. "I'm certain our good boniface will tell me everything we need to know."

"We stand ready to serve the public in any—"

"Someone most important to us has been lost. We've been searching the countryside for hours, inquiring at inns and—"

"Say no more, sir." Hogg smiled broadly. "I can put your distraught and troubled minds to rest, for the very person you seek slumbers at this very moment within the sturdy walls of the Martyr."

The visitor let go of him. "Ah, she's here, then, is she?"

"That she is."

"We'll be, if you have no objections, taking her off with us."

Hogg frowned briefly. "I wonder, sir, if the night air will be at all salubrious for the old darling. A woman of her quite advanced years must surely be in a delicate state of—"

"Advanced years?" The man took hold of the front of Hogg again.

The innkeeper's eyes widened. "Is it not the kind-faced old grandmother you seek, gentlemen?" he inquired in a puzzled tone. "Why, from the moment the dear old person came tottering into the Martyr I felt, and I communicated as much to Mrs. Hogg, a fine figure of a woman, I might add, who agreed that—"

"We want a *young* girl. Young and comely, with copper-colored hair."

"Do you indeed?" Hogg shook his head sadly. "Then what's to become of this gentle soul? I remarked soon as I set eyes on her, eyes noted far and wide for the accurateness of perception, she was a much agitated and upset old person. I surmised she'd perhaps quarreled with her loved ones and come rushing out into—"

"Listen to me," roared the man, tugging Hogg close to him. "It is a *young* girl with *red* hair we're after. Have you seen her this night?"

"Why, no," answered Hogg. "I assumed you were in quest of your misplaced and wandering grandmother who—"

"My grandmother sells vegetables on the streets of London and were I never to see the old crone in this lifetime again it would do naught but please me." He shoved Hogg away from him. "You've wasted a good deal of our time with your foolish babbling."

"I count no time wasted which is spent in pleasant discourse, sir."

"Should a girl such as I've described appear here later on, old man, see to it you hold her. We'll no doubt, should we not find her elsewhere tonight, stop in to visit you on the morrow."

"You're always welcome at the Martyr, sir. All and sundry weary travelers think of it as a haven—"

"Good night to you." The man made a snarling noise, turned on his booted heel, and hurried back to his horse.

"May your hunt be successful, gentlemen," called Hogg as they went galloping out of his courtyard and into the darkness of the night. He remained in the open doorway for a moment, a satisfied smile growing on his lips. "I shan't be turning her over to you, my friends. Not a bit of it. I've other plans for that young lady."

Chapter 20

She sat suddenly upright, heart pounding against her ribs.

It was not a dream that had awakened Alicia.

The door to her room, the door she'd locked from the inside before retiring, had swung open.

Framed in a rectangle of flickering yellow light were three figures. As the frightened girl watched, the figures moved out of the doorway and into her room.

One of them was Sebastian Hogg. He came first, candle held high and a quirked smile on his broad face. The man behind him she had never seen before, a huge swarthy fellow in a shabby greatcoat. The third intruder was a woman, skinny and slovenly.

"No time for you to dress, pretty, so get this on

you." The thin woman shuffled over to the bed and threw a frayed cloak to her. "Hurry now, we've not all that much time."

Having no night things, Alicia had gone to bed in her undergarments. She picked up the musty-smelling garment and held it to the front of her. "What's the meaning of this?" she asked, directing her question to the smiling innkeeper.

"We have, I must ruefully admit, a few sidelines here at the Martyr, necessitated in the main by the somewhat unstable state of the economy due to—"

"Get up, put on that cloak," the thin woman interrupted. "Let's be going!"

"Going where?"

"Why, to London, miss," said Hogg.

Alicia moved until her slim back was pressing against the wall. "You told me there was no way to journey there until morning."

"That was before we decided we could make use of you," the thin woman told her. All at once she grabbed Alicia by the wrist, pulled her off balance, and slapped her hard across the cheek. "We've had more than enough talk. Get up out of there at once, or I'll have Busino drag you out."

"Now, my dear," cautioned Hogg. "We don't wish to give this young lady a completely bad impression of us. There's no need to—"

"She'll get plenty of rough treatment if she don't behave when she gets to Madam Cornucopia's."

"I'm not going anywhere against my will," insisted Alicia. "Least of all to any Madam Cornucopia's. It sounds like . . . like . . ."

"It's exactly that, pretty," said Mrs. Hogg. "A house of ill fame. Hogg and I have long and profitably supplied young ladies, willing and otherwise, to the establishment."

"Economic conditions being in such a sorry state," began Hogg, "we've found it necessary—"

"No need to explain and apologize, Hogg," said his thin wife. "We have to hurry and be away from here before them others return."

"Others?" said Alicia.

"A pair of brutish fellows," said Hogg. "Raised a terrible to-do in looking for you, hunting you as fervently as a pack of dogs follows the trail of Brother Reynard. You must be quite important to them."

"I come from a very important and influential family," the girl told him. "I warn you, should you—"

"No one will ever find you at Madam C's," Mrs. Hogg assured her.

"My family would certainly be willing to pay you to—"

"Much too risky, I fear," said Hogg, with a shake of his head. "Attempting to collect a fat ransom usually ends one on the gallows. This way we make a lesser profit but we live to spend and benefit from—"

"Come along now." The thin woman yanked the protesting girl from the bed and shoved her against the wall.

"Quite a comely lass," remarked the swarthy Busino, chuckling.

"There's no need for rude remarks, Busino," warned Hogg.

His wife snatched up the old cloak, draped it unceremoniously around Alicia's shivering shoulders, and said, "Bring the gag, Busino."

"Got it right here in me pocket." He shambled

closer, producing a dirty length of foul-smelling cloth.

Alicia recoiled. "No, I won't let you!" She slapped at the lean face of Mrs. Hogg.

The thin woman dodged, delivered a hard blow to the girl's face. "No more of this now, pretty. I don't want you too damaged afore we make delivery."

"I'll never allow you to—" Alicia lunged, head low, and butted into the older woman's chest. Then she attempted to slip around her and reach the open doorway.

Mrs. Hogg, cursing, dived and caught hold of the girl's bare arm. She tugged her back, spun her around, and hit her again in the face.

"My dear, be cautious," said Hogg. "Lest you . . ."

Alicia heard no more. The scene before her vanished like the flame of a snuffed candle. She fell to the hard floor unconscious.

". . . ought not to do it."

"Davey, me lad, I don't wish to smack your noddle," the gruff Busino was saying. "Yet I surely will if you stop not this foolishness."

Alicia found herself propped within the cab of a musty carriage. Her wrists and ankles were tightly tied; the filthy strip of cloth was tied cross her mouth and cutting into her flesh.

The carriage still stood in the courtyard of the Martyr's Head Inn. Outside in the chill predawn darkness Busino was arguing with the kitchen boy Alicia had met on her arrival.

"She's much too fine a lady to—"

"Enough," growled Busino. "Now help me get

these bloody reins untangled. I've got to leave for London before too many more minutes pass."

"If you take her," threatened Davey, "I'll fly to the sheriff in—"

The sound of a slap.

"You breathe so much as a word of what's taken place this night, my lad, and you'll find yourself with a sliced throat. I promise you."

Davey said no more.

Alicia struggled, but the cords which held her wrists and ankles were tight and secure. Tugging, attempting to pry her wrists even a fraction apart succeeded only in causing her pain.

"There, all's in readiness," announced Busino. "Back to your bed now, Davey. I'm set to—"

Busino never got to complete his sentence. Instead he produced an odd sighing noise.

Alicia twisted, leaned, and managed to get a glimpse of what was happening out in the courtyard.

She saw Busino, shaking his head groggily, rising up off the mismatched flagstones. Standing over him was a lithe figure, watchful, fists at the ready.

It was Rob.

The swarthy man attempted to rise again. Kilgerrin hit him.

He fell.

One more try, two more smashing blows.

Busino sank for good.

Kilgerrin watched the sprawled body for a few seconds, then came sprinting to the carriage.

"Look out, sir," cried Davey as Kilgerrin reached for the handle of the carriage door.

Kilgerrin spun. When he faced the landlord, who'd just come running out of the inn, there was a sturdy pistol in his fist.

Hogg carried a pistol, too.

"I can promise you I am a far better shot than you, sir," Kilgerrin informed the innkeeper in a level voice. "I suggest you discard your weapon and spare me the trouble of killing you where you stand."

Hogg hesitated, swallowing hard. Then he let the gun fall from his hand to the flagstones. "As you say," he murmured.

Cautiously, pistol still ready, Kilgerrin opened the carriage. From inside his cloak he drew a clasp knife. "Boy . . . Davey, is it? Come here and cut this lady's bonds."

"Right you are, sir."

"Yes, go right ahead," said Hogg, attempting a smile. "Under the circumstances, I shan't consider it disloyal for you to—"

Pivoting, Kilgerrin fired his pistol.

A window on the first floor of the inn shattered; a woman screamed.

"Throw down that blunderbuss, madam," called Kilgerrin. "And make no further attempts to use me as a target."

"Mortally wounded," moaned Mrs. Hogg. "I fear I am mortally wounded."

"Throw it down at once, or I'll come up there and toss the both of you into the courtyard," Kilgerrin told her.

Hogg said, "Sir, you ought not to address a member of the fair sex in such a rude and—"

"You," Kilgerrin warned the innkeeper, "I'll skewer and leave you roasting on the spit if you interrupt me once again."

Davey, recovered from the latest surprise and shock, came running. He took the proffered knife and used it to good advantage.

Before he had the gag away from Alicia's mouth, the blunderbuss came sailing out of the ruined window.

"I'm giving up the ghost," wailed Mrs. Hogg.

"Might I at least administer to my dear wife in her last—"

"Silence!" suggested Kilgerrin. He glanced in at Alicia. "Are you well enough to ride?"

"Oh, yes, Rob, I'm fine."

"Good. Then we'll borrow a horse for you and take our leave."

"I do hope, sir," said Hogg, "you won't allow this little incident to spoil your opinion of the Martyr's Head."

"You can discuss that with the magistrates before long," said Kilgerrin. He reached into the dark carriage and, with one strong arm, lifted the girl out.

She asked, "How did you—"

"Explanations will come later," he promised. "First we must get you safely away from here."

"I'll saddle our best mount for you," offered Davey in a low voice.

"Thank you," said Alicia, smiling for the first time in many hours.

Chapter 21

He carried her across the threshold.

The hall was dark and hollow-feeling. Kilgerrin, gently, placed Alicia on her feet.

"That wasn't exactly necessary," she said softly. "I'm perfectly capable of—"

Kilgerrin kissed her, then said, "Stay precisely where you are for a moment."

She heard him striding away into the surrounding blackness. A flint was struck, and a candle blossomed into life.

The hallway was large, the walls paneled in dark wood, the floor richly carpeted. "Is this your country house?" the girl inquired.

"No, that of a friend," Kilgerrin replied while lighting another candle. "I am a guest here occasionally and have permission to stop in whenever I chance to be in the vicinity. Since it lies only a few miles from the Martyr's Head, it seemed a good place to seek sanctuary for the night."

She looked around her. "Are there no servants?"

"Only the old fellow whom I awakened out at the caretaker's cottage," said Kilgerrin, grinning. "I fear we'll be unattended and unchaperoned, Alicia."

"It's not that I was thinking of," she said, lowering her eyes. "I was simply puzzled to find no one rushing to inquire who was invading their household at such a strange hour."

"Must be nearly dawn, at that." Kilgerrin took hold of his watch fob, tugged out his timepiece. "Yes, nearly five."

"I am not at all, surprisingly, tired or drowsy," she told him. "Mayn't we sit up and talk? There's a great deal that's happened to me in the day just passed."

The young man turned his back to her and concentrated on lighting the candles in a three-prong holder. "Wouldn't you rather wait until morning?"

"I would not."

Facing her, smiling, he said, "Very well, talk we shall. First, however, I do think we'd better concern ourselves with the matter of getting you properly dressed."

Alicia glanced down at the ragged cloak which clothed her. It had added a glaze of road dust during their gallop to this untenanted country house. "I'm afraid my own clothes are lost," she said. "Even my supply of money is—"

"Your coin purse is safe." Kilgerrin extracted it from his coat pocket and placed it on a small table. "Young Davey managed to retrieve it for you from the person of the fellow I stretched out on the flag-stones."

"A very nice and thoughtful boy."

"Surprisingly honest, as well, considering his surroundings." Kilgerrin nodded at a curving staircase which rose away from them up into the shadows of the next floor. "Once, not that long ago, there were two young ladies in residence here. Both are now, and relatively happily so, married and gone. I believe they left some garments behind. They may not be in the height of fashion, Alicia, yet they should serve."

The girl smiled at him. "We may safely ignore fashion for now."

Kilgerrin picked up the candlestick. "Allow me to lead you to a room," he offered. "Then I'll see what I can do about finding you a gown or two."

"One will be sufficient." She took hold of his arm and they climbed the stairs together. "These young ladies were relatives of yours, perhaps?"

"Not kin at all, no."

"Ah, then perhaps you courted one . . . or both?"

"Neither, although the pair of them were ravishingly beautiful," he told her. "Yes, ravishingly lovely, and the both of them head over heels in love with me. I, for my part, scorned them. The reason being that many years ago at a humble town fair a squint-eyed gypsy woman had peered into my palm and prophesied I'd someday meet a lovely auburn-haired lass whose first name started with the letter A. I made up my mind then and there to ignore the blandishments of all other women until I met—"

"Abigail Smedley."

Kilgerrin cleared his throat. "Now that you men-

117

tion it, Alicia, the girl did have a head of hair of a somewhat reddish cast, didn't she? Always struck me as more carroty than auburn."

"It was auburn, Abigail's hair, a shade quite similar to mine," she said. "From what I've heard whispered behind fans at various London social functions, you and the lovely Abbie got along quite famously for a time."

"Well, that's what I get for listening to old one-eyed fortune-tellers." He opened the door they'd reached. It was a large and well-appointed bedchamber. Kilgerrin crossed, placed the candles on a bedside table. "Will this do, mum?"

"Quite well." She did a slow spin, taking in all the details of the room. "One might even class it as lavish."

"A bit dusty." He ran a finger along the marble mantelpiece, raising a few tiny gray flecks.

"I can remedy that."

"Wait here, then," he said, "while I go search you out a temporary wardrobe."

"Anything at all serviceable will do, Rob."

"But it must match your famed auburn tresses," he said. Smiling and bowing slightly, he left her.

Alicia made a casual circuit of the room. She stopped beside the canopied bed and, unfastening the worn cloak, sat on the bed's edge.

She'd told Rob she was very anxious to discuss all that had happened, which was true. She did feel, now she sat and considered, very sleepy after all. Perhaps if she just stretched out atop the coverlet for a few . . .

Chapter 22

Sunlight everywhere.

Flooding in through the high windows, filling the immense bedroom.

Alicia found herself beneath a large quilt. She sat up, looked around.

A chair had been moved close to the bed, and draped over it were three frocks. Smiling to herself, she slipped out of bed. Atop the marble-top commode she found a bowl and a pitcher filled with fresh water.

Pinned to the wall immediately above the bowl was a note. *I'll be on the terrace when you awaken. I am prepared to concoct a perfectly acceptable breakfast should that be necessary. Love, Rob.*

Stretching out her hand, Alicia ran her fingertips over the note.

She found him sitting on a stone railing, gazing out at the vast park which stretched away for acres and acres beyond the great house. After a few hundred yards the landscape grew increasingly wild; nature was quietly reclaiming the once well-groomed estate grounds.

"What do you think?"

He turned, studied her. "You look absolutely splendid," was his judgment. "I feel vindicated."

She touched her fingers to the low-cut bodice. "All three frocks are very fine."

"While not being an expert in the area, I nevertheless tried to envision you in each of the gowns," explained the handsome Kilgerrin. "An exercise which took considerably longer than—"

"Are you certain, Rob, you didn't remain away until I'd fallen safely asleep?"

He grinned. "Well, perhaps I did feel you needed rest more than conversation."

Sighing softly, she asked, "What time has it gotten to be?"

"Approaching noon." He stood. "I actually did learn a bit about the culinary arts from a very loyal cook who served my late Uncle Jackeen for—"

"A demonstration of your gifts in the scullery can wait, Rob. More important is the conversation we were to have had last evening."

"After an ordeal such as you've suffered, Alicia, food is part of the prescribed—"

"Can it be you're trying to avoid a discussion?" She walked purposefully toward him.

"Not at all." He took her hand. "There's a most comfortable bench down in the garden yonder. Shall we sit there and—"

"Right here will serve." She perched herself on

120

the railing of stone. "Now then. How did you come to be at that dreadful inn last night?"

"I was searching for you," he replied. "I'd tried several other inns and places of lodging, seeking some clue. I chanced to arrive at the Martyr in time to see that loutish chap carrying you out of the inn and depositing you in that carriage."

"Rob, they were going to . . . sell me to some horrible woman in London."

"Yes, I know the kind of business Hogg engages in on the side."

Alicia asked, "How did you know to come looking for me at all?"

"I knew when I left London that you were being taken to Ravenshaw Court, or at least I suspected as much," he said. "I set out to catch up with you. I followed the most obvious route and some time after nightfall I caught up with the carriage you'd been traveling in."

"Aunt Elizabeth . . . is she . . . ?"

"In absolutely top form, she and Dante were both protesting most vociferously when I encountered them at the Black Swan Inn, some three miles beyond the place where you were originally set upon," he said. "Your driver's wound was trifling, and he was able to get the vehicle as far as the Black Swan before taking to his bed and calling for a sawbones."

"How did you know where I might be?"

"All I knew was, according to your much agitated aunt, you'd fled into the forest during the highwaymen's attack. She'd been unable to find a trace of you and decided to withdraw to the nearest inn. I imagine she's mounting, with the possible aid of your Uncle Tobias, a searching party for you by now."

"Rob," said Alicia, "I am near certain she knew those men who waylaid us."

"Yes, that's quite probable. I have a good idea who employed them."

She placed her other hand over his and pressed. "They meant to kill me, you know."

"Yes."

"Do you know why?"

Kilgerrin frowned. "Alicia, there are things afoot . . . because of the conflict and the power of a man like Napoleon . . ." He paused, struggling to order his thoughts and trying to decide how much to confide in the girl. "Very well, it's my opinion you are in the possession of some information which others feel is harmful to them."

"That simply is not so, Rob. I swear to you I know nothing that might prompt anyone to wish my death."

"We'll come to that in a moment," he said. "The point is, certain people in this country are working to aid Bonaparte's cause and—"

"I still do not see what this has to do with me."

"I am very much afraid your Uncle Tobias and your Aunt Elizabeth are involved in the business of spying for France."

The girl inhaled sharply. "That's ridiculous, impossible. You can't be—"

"You yourself told me you thought she knew the men who attacked your carriage."

"Yes, but—"

"She does indeed know them. They are, almost beyond a doubt, in the pay of Lord Cranford."

The girl shook her head slowly from side to side. "Why on earth would Lord Cranford want me killed?"

"Because the man is deeply involved in betraying England to the French."

"And you actually think Aunt Elizabeth and my Uncle Toby are working with him?"

"I do, yes."

"That would mean Aunt Elizabeth allowed me to ride into that trap. That she knew I would be killed and did nothing to prevent it."

"No, that isn't, in my opinion, the case," Kilgerrin said. "Your aunt and uncle have other plans for you, plans involving Dr. Noah Marryat."

"Marryat?" She shuddered. "Why does that dreadful little man keep coming into this?"

"He's linked with Cranford and the Bonaparte sympathizers," Kilgerrin said. "You must know Dr. Marryat is noted for his ability as a mesmerist. Alicia, he must have practiced his art on you at some point."

She paled, vehemently shaking her head. "No, he never . . . Oh, Rob, I'm not at all sure. Sometimes I think . . . it's all tangled up." She pressed one hand to her temple. "Images of that awful wrinkled face and those burning eyes . . . and Ravenshaw Court and . . . a pistol . . . and my . . ." She threw her arms around him, pressed her head hard against his broad chest. "I'm the one who wanted to talk of this, yet now I find I can't."

"We'll abandon the subject for now."

"Sooner or late, Rob, I must . . . sort out all my thoughts. They seem so tangled."

"I'll help you."

"And . . . I'm not used to people wanting to take my life."

"No one will do that, you've no more to fear," he promised.

Chapter 23

"Just notice how tragic and downcast he seems. He's quite given up the idea of eating, instead he wastes away. Can you suggest something which might—"

"Madam, I do not treat livestock."

"By Jove, Liz, this is no time to worry us all over that miserable dog."

Aunt Elizabeth stiffened in her chair. "It is entirely your fault Dante suffered as he did, Tobias," she accused her nephew. "The least—"

"Damnation, woman." Copplestone hit at his desk with his fist, causing his inkstand to hop. "How many times must I swear this to you? I had naught to do with the waylaying of that carriage."

Dr. Marryat was sitting nearest the library fireplace. He stuffed a substantial pinch of snuff into one of his nostrils, sniffed, smiled, and gave out a formidable sneeze. "This bickering," he then pointed out, "does nothing toward solving our major problem."

Elizabeth ignored the withered little mesmerist. "Why else would Lord Cranford have sent his underlings to assault me and poor lost Alicia? I recognized one of them instantly. Tobias, you must certainly have—"

"Damnation!" repeated the angry nephew. "Was I the only one who knew you and the girl were coming here?"

The old woman adjusted her lace cap, then rubbed tenderly at the head of the forlorn Dante, who lay sprawled across her narrow lap. "Yes, you knew of our journey also, doctor."

Marryat sneezed. "Madam, I traveled all the way from London, and a most unpleasant, dull, and bone-rattling trip it was, so I might treat this miserable niece of yours," he said. "Had I assumed she was going to be murdered en route, I'd have spared myself the rigors of the trip here, I assure you."

"It doesn't matter how Lord Cranford found out." Copplestone left his desk to begin pacing around the library. "Obviously he has heard somehow that Alicia may remember what she saw here . . . on that awful night."

"Very little Lord Cranford doesn't hear," remarked Dr. Marryat, applying snuff to his other nostril.

"He agreed to let us handle this matter our way," persisted Elizabeth. "Taking action on his own very much indicates bad faith on his part."

Marryat sneezed profoundly. "I believe the long-awaited invasion of these shores by the forces of the glorious Napoleon Bonaparte grows ever closer."

"What?" Copplestone stopped dead. "Why wasn't I informed of—"

"I am informing you now, sir," said the little doctor. "It may well be Lord Cranford doesn't want to risk exposure of any one of us at such a critical time."

"The invasion, everything we've been working for . . . it's finally to come?"

Nodding slowly, Dr. Marryat said, "I personally feel the life of one foolish girl doesn't mean much to Lord Cranford. We all of us have long known we'd have to make many sacrifices in order to—"

"She won't be killed!" cried Elizabeth. "No!"

Startled, Dante rose up and leaped to the floor.

"The cause," said Marryat, turning his gleaming little eyes on the old woman. "The cause must always come before personal feelings, madam."

"Alicia's not to be slaughtered," said the old woman stubbornly. "I believe in what we're about as much as any one; I know full well that as long as that fat fool rules England there'll be no—"

"You are going to have to be prepared to make even greater sacrifices than the life of this young woman," cut in the doctor. "May I remind you that you had no objection to the out-and-out murder of her father. We all three connived at that, we all readily entered into the scheme to cover that murder up and make it seem a natural death." He pointed a snuff-daubed finger first at her and then at Copplestone. "The truth of the matter is, you allowed Alicia to be hypnotized out of all memory of what she'd seen. And what she saw, sir, was you shooting down your own brother."

Copplestone swayed, clutching at his side. "God forgive me, I did."

"That seemed expedient at the time," said Aunt Elizabeth calmly. "Otherwise, since he'd unfortunately learned what we were about, he might well have betrayed us to the Regent and the Secret Service."

"My own brother," murmured Copplestone, sinking into a wing chair. "Had there only been some other way to—"

"There wasn't," Marryat told him. "There really isn't at present, either. Stand aside, allow Lord Cranford to do what must be done. We're playing for extremely high stakes in this game."

"You claim to be the best hypnotist in all of England, doctor," the old woman said. "You have always maintained you could erase all memory of witnessing the murder of her father from the girl's mind. For a time it appeared you had succeeded; now it seems otherwise. Yet you boast you can still expunge these memories which are fighting their way back into her consciousness."

"Most assuredly I can," said the little doctor. "In order to affect such a cure, however, I must have the girl. She is, need I point out, most noticeably and completely missing."

"Tobias," instructed the old woman, "you'll go at once to Lord Cranford and inform him he is to leave Alicia completely alone henceforth. I, meanwhile, will supervise the search for the poor child from here at Ravenshaw Court. You, Dr. Marryat, shall remain here until we find her and—"

"I have my practice to consider, madam, not to mention my work for our mutual cause. London is where I ought to be even now."

"Aunt Liz," protested her nephew, "Cranford happens to be a most powerful man. I sincerely doubt he'll listen to me."

"He had very well better listen to you, or he may regret it."

"Are you," asked Dr. Marryat as he rose out of his chair, "threatening Lord Cranford?"

"Not yet," she said.

Chapter 24

Alicia stroked the stem of the wineglass, then took a sip of the deep red liquid within. "This is," she said softly, eyes on the fireplace and the glowing logs, "the first completely happy day I've spent in a long while, Rob."

"The first of many." He was standing near the fire, elbow resting on the marble mantelpiece. His glass of port sat untouched near an ornate candlestick.

From her chair the girl said, "I seem to sense a restlessness in you, you're like some charger anxious to be galloping across open fields."

He grinned. "Inaction right now does unsettle me," he admitted. "There are a great many things I must do, to insure your safety."

"We're safe here," she said.

Nodding, Kilgerrin strode to the window. Night had already taken hold of the grounds of the estate. "I've sent for my man, Rumsford," he said.

"Oh, so? To serve as a chaperone, perhaps?"

"To look after you." He faced her. "No one can touch you here and, I hope, before very long Lord Cranford and his followers will no longer be in any position to bother you."

"You honestly believe . . . that Aunt Elizabeth and my Uncle Toby . . . are guilty of treason."

"At the very least, yes," he replied. "I must get back to London to set various things in motion. As soon as good Rumsford arrives, I'm afraid I must leave you for a few days."

"When will he appear, do you think?"

"Not before tomorrow."

"Well, then, we still have tonight to ourselves."

Kilgerrin crossed, knelt beside her chair. "I do love you, Alicia," he said quietly. "No matter what may happen in the course of the next few weeks, hold fast to that fact."

After placing her glass aside, she touched his cheek with her fingertips, then the hair which curled around his temples. "You act as though you, too, carry around some dark and awful secret, Rob."

His eyes met hers. "I am keeping nothing important back from you."

"Yet you seem so weighed down by something."

"Chiefly by my concern for you, and my anger at those who've tried to hurt you." Taking hold of the hand which caressed his cheek, he kissed her fingertips.

"The two of us here, alone and close," she said very softly. "If only that could go on and on."

He stood, pulled her gently to her feet, and

took her in his strong arms. "It will go on, Alicia, I swear. As soon as this business is at an end."

She locked her arms around his neck and kissed him. Then finally she said, "I'm afraid of tonight . . . of being alone."

"You won't be alone tonight," he said.

He wasn't there.

Alicia opened her eyes on the morning bed-chamber. Bright sunlight had invaded the room. She was alone in the wide canopy bed.

Naked, she sat up and stretched, making a contented murmuring sound.

It was a beautiful day and she was immensely happy, even though she and Rob would be parting within a very few hours. She knew with a warm and satisfying certainty the separation could only be temporary.

". . . *not* tell her!"

An unfamiliar voice, loud, coming from somewhere in the house.

She slipped out of bed and clothed herself hurriedly in a dressing gown.

The voice sounded angry. Could Rob be in some kind of danger?

Silently, Alicia opened the door of her room.

They were in the library on the ground floor, voices somewhat lowered now. Rob and another man arguing.

She hesitated at the head of the stairs, hand twisting at the carved newel post. Then she quietly began to descend the staircase.

The door of the library was ajar and from the long hall she could hear what was being said inside. Pressing against the dark paneling, between two scowling ancestral portraits, she stopped to eavesdrop.

". . . she's in very great danger, Lord Mac," Rob was saying.

That would be Lord MacQuarrie he was arguing with. She'd met the man in London, never liked him. She knew he was a friend of Rob's, perhaps the very friend to whom this grand house belonged. Was he angry over their intrusion?

"I am very much aware of the gravity of the situation," Lord MacQuarrie said.

"Then allow me to tell her the whole story. I cannot go on acting out this deceitful role."

"No, it's impossible. She knows far too much as it is."

"But, Lord Mac, they mean to kill her! The more she knows, the better able she'll be to—"

"I tell you, man, you cannot."

"And if I defy you?"

Lord MacQuarrie said, "Would you really tell Alicia Kingsley everything, Rob? Tell her that you were *ordered* to pay court to her so you might gain information about the treasonous activities of her uncle? Do you really wish to inform the girl you are nothing more than a spy hired to . . ."

The sunlight went away. Everything became very cold. Alicia heard nothing for a moment except the sudden incredibly loud beating of her heart. She put out one hand, pressed the palm against the wall. The wave of dizziness passed; she did not fall.

Silently she turned away and went swiftly back up to the bedchamber.

"He doesn't care for me . . . he was ordered to do this . . . he doesn't love me at all. . . ."

Very quickly, not aware of the motions, she

dressed herself in the borrowed clothes. Then she left the room, hurried down the back stairway.

There were horses in the stables, she knew that. In her hand she clutched the coin purse.

She selected a roan mare, saddled it expertly, moving like an automaton as she did.

Less than fifteen minutes after she'd learned the truth, she was riding away from the great house and from, so she believed, Rob Kilgerrin forever.

Chapter 25

Market day in the village of Middlesworth. A bright and warm afternoon, the streets and lanes and rows crowded with people from the surrounding countryside. The bow-windowed shops were doing brisk business, as were the stalls and even the handbarrows. Everywhere there was a clutter of shoppers and goods for sale.

Alicia, slightly dusty from her ride, stood near the grassy town square beside the small stone bridge which arches over Middlesworth's most prominent stream. There were ducks and swans gliding on the blue waters, as well as a fleet of toy boats being propelled from the mossy shore by sticks, poles, and tangles of twine. Crossing the bridge, most slowly and reluctantly, were a half-dozen milk cows. They were being guided by a grizzled farmer in a much-patched smock to the cattle market to be held in one of the village's narrowest streets. Their hooves clacked on the stones of the bridge, their mournful lowing drifted out across the sunny square.

At a spot nearly a mile outside of Middlesworth, just beyond the fingerpost announcing the fact that the village was nearby, Alicia had dismounted and, with a hefty slap on its flanks, sent her horse galloping off the way they'd come. With any luck it would take itself back to Lord MacQuarrie's stables by sundown today. Now there was nothing to link her with the place, or with Rob Kilgerrin.

She was not the kind to cry. But when she thought of how Rob had lied, she very nearly did burst into tears.

"That'll do you not a bit of good," she reminded herself.

Standing there near the center of this pleasant village, surrounded by activity and mostly happy people, the girl took stock of her situation.

She had a little less than three pounds in her coin purse, enough to last awhile if she husbanded the money wisely enough. She also had the frock she was wearing, not actually hers but it could be counted a possession. And that was very nearly all.

True, others had started out alone with less in the way of worldly goods. Most of them, the humble beginners who'd risen to great heights, had been men. For a lone and friendless girl, the situation loomed much bleaker. The days ahead would be very rough indeed. There was, as well, the danger she might find herself pressed into enployment for someone like Madam Cornucopia. Or worse.

"I must be very careful."

She would not, she vowed, turn back. She'd

never go to Rob for help again, nor would she go near her aunt and uncle. That part of her life was over and done.

Alicia started to walk across the stone bridge, admitting inwardly she had no clear idea of what she would do next. The past few days her main goals had been to get free of unpleasant situations. Away from those who meant to kill her, from those who wanted to sell her into a life of shame. And away from Rob Kilgerrin, who'd proved to be completely false.

Yes, she had a very strong and clear idea of what she was running from. Yet not a glimmer of what she was running to.

"I must simply drift with the current for a while. Like those fragile little boats down there."

A juggler was cavorting at the edge of the green, keeping five silver globes spinning and flashing in the afternoon sunlight. Near him a plump pieman offered some quite tempting wares.

The girl realized she hadn't eaten since last evening. Last evening when everything had been so splendid, when she and Rob had . . . There was no use thinking of that, of the tenderness and affection she'd believed existed between them. That was over, dead.

After her experience at the Martyr's Head she was a shade reluctant to enter an inn alone and order a meal for herself. She walked for a time, gazing, though not really seeing, into shop windows and listening to the cries of the street vendors. The pitchmen's calls, the laughter of children, the bargaining of customers and tradesmen, all of it blended into a pleasant undertone.

The front of the Yellow Lion Inn was freshly painted a color to match the name on its sign. The bow-windows gleamed, and inside Alicia could see several reputable folk dining at some of the oaken tables. She decided to chance ordering a simple meal.

The dining room smelled of roasting meat, fresh-drawn ale, and spices. A small wiry man with vast amounts of crinkly gray hair encircling his prominent ears and none at all atop his skull introduced himself as proprietor of the Yellow Lion and guided Alicia to a small table in a quiet corner.

While she awaited the chop she'd ordered from the grill, Alicia studied her fellow patrons unobtrusively. The occupants of a large, and festive, table across the beam-ceilinged room especially drew her interest.

Presiding, and that was the exact word for it, over the group was a handsome, though slightly red-faced and overweight, man of fifty-odd years. He was dressed in the style of somewhat earlier times, with a velvet-collared coat, a striped satin waistcoat, and knee breeches. His voice was deep and resonant, and fragments of his conversation reached Alicia through the noise and bustle of the dining room.

". . . a perpetual feast of nectared sweets, where no crude surfeit reigns . . ."

Seated to the right of this gentleman was a once-beautiful woman in her waning thirties. Her hair had remained—though perhaps nature was now aided a bit—a raven black, and her skin was a milky white. A few wrinkles and a puffiness beneath the eyes robbed the face of some of its former beauty. She was very attentive to the presiding gentleman, nodding at the aptness of his quotes, smiling at his frequent jests.

Opposite her sat, or rather perched, an enormous man who appeared to be inflated by some lighter-than-air substance almost to the bursting point. Alicia wondered whether he would explode or simply float out of his chair at any moment. He favored colors of bright hue, his frock coat was bottle-green, his waistcoat the color of the sky on a spring day, his cravat a dazzling yellow. His abundant hair, which was a gleaming orange, topped off his rainbow ensemble.

The final occupant of the table aroused the girl's curiosity the most. He was a relatively young man, no more than five and twenty she guessed. His face, though, was most changeable. One moment he would have a long nose and pointed chin, yet when she looked again the nose would be broad and flat, the chin almost nonexistent.

". . . yon fair maiden is the answer to all our fretful prayers," the leader of the party said.

The raven-haired woman smiled, shifted very slightly in her chair until she was gazing directly across at Alicia. "Yes, I quite agree, Josh."

Alicia tried not to blush. Apparently they were aware she'd been gaping at them. She busied herself with her meal.

"Digby," suggested the man who was apparently named Joshua, "cease swallowing your nose and apply yourself to acting as Hermes."

"Last one was toppin', eh?" inquired young Digby, his face settling into a new mold. "All done with art and skill, not a bit of paint or false hair. Merely by manipulatin' my pliable features I can assume the—"

"Digby, the task at hand is to recruit the maiden fair."

The young man rubbed his palm over his face. "Have I my original frontispiece on, Valerie?"

"Close enough as don't matter, Dig," the woman replied.

A throat-clearing and a polite clicking of booted heels informed Alicia someone was now hovering over her table.

She raised her eyes and saw the young man with the changeable face smiling down at her.

"Miss, permit me to intrude on your privacy and introduce myself to you," he said in a voice quite unlike the one he'd been using previously. "I have the pleasure of being, at least so far as my vast and doting public is concerned, none other than Digby Grand."

"Yes?"

Digby bowed deeply, his blond head nearly touching the table top. Straightening, smile broadening, he announced, "I have been deputized to inform you your future is henceforth secure."

Chapter 26

". . . or mayhap an heiress fleeing an unscrupulous and machinating stepfather. Yet again you might well be the dowerless and only child of a penniless but good-hearted squire, escaping on the eve of an enforced and loveless union with a Croesus-like but otherwise loathsome suitor. There is also a possibility you've been cast out because of the ascendance of a young and cold-blooded stepmother, sent forth into the teeth of a raging blizzard, nipped at by the jagged claws of—"

"Josh, it hasn't snowed in this part of England since last March."

"Ah, you are absolutely right, Valerie. My teeming brain quite o'er ran itself," said Joshua Cardwell. "Perhaps you'll save me further effusions, dear child, and explain your present circumstances yourself."

"I'd rather," Alicia told him, "not."

They were in a small and not too well-lit meeting hall. Alicia had accompanied Joshua Cardwell and his group here, somewhat reluctantly and after considerable persuasion, from the Yellow Lion Inn. Cardwell had stationed himself up on the small stage while the rest remained below.

"A woman of mystery," said Digby, scratching at his straw-colored thatch. "We've not had such in the company since Lady . . . well, I'd best not breathe her name."

From the stage Cardwell said, opening his gloved hands wide, "Makes no difference, lass, from whence ye've come. Be it marbled palace or dank hovel, we'd all like to have you join the Cardwell Tragic & Comic Traveling Theater company. When we espied you in the Yellow Lion I knew the at last kindly gods had sent me exactly—"

"I wonder if there's any possible way," said Alicia, "that I could be of—"

"We find ourselves in the most sincere and desperate need of a young lady to join us," said the actor-manager. "A week ago, and well do I recall the fateful eve, our fair specialist in maidenly roles most unexpectedly and unceremoniously resigned to enter into what I confidently forecast will be a most disastrous marital union with a corpulent and ageing man of trade who lends his far from proud name to a swill glorying under the title of Stowbridge's Best Ale."

"I've had to double in many of the young lady parts," added Digby. "Which ain't, despite my considerable skills as a mimic, set well with some of our more rustic audiences."

Valerie moved closer to the girl, put a friendly

hand on her shoulder. "No doubt you've heard many lurid tales about the life and habits of itinerant actors," she said. "You'll find those of us who travel with Josh to be a decent and upright collection of folk."

"Honest and clean," put in the multicolored balloon-like man, who'd been introduced to her earlier as Will Bascom.

"You'll do yourself and your good reputation no harm should you join us," said Valerie.

"The salary, as mentioned earlier, is not magnificent, yet it is sufficient," said Cardwell from the small stage. "The work is only moderately taxing. We tour during the more clement months and our repertoire consists of a most satisfying and illuminating potpourri of the most brilliant works of Britain's bards, a judicious combination of the antic and the sublime, the grim and the farcical. This season, to give you a pertinent example, we shall be doing *Macbeth, The Duchess of Malfi, The Knight of the Burning Pestle, She Stoops to Conquer, The Revenger's Tragedy,* and *'Tis Pity She's a Whore.*" He paused, moved close to the stage edge, and knelt on one knee. "We are scheduled to open on the morrow for three magnificent days in this benighted community. We begin with *The Tragical History of Ronald I,* and I swear, dear girl, you'd make a perfect Francesca."

"I've never performed in my life," said Alicia. "But as you've all surmised . . . I am a runaway and most urgently in need of some kind of honest employment."

"There is a tide in men's affairs, and in the affairs of young women, too, for that matter," Cardwell told her. "Now is the time, my dear Alicia, to plunge."

"If you'll work diligently with me from now until tomorrow eve," promised Valerie, "I'll see you give a creditable if not brilliant performance in the play."

"Oh, I've no fear your could teach me the lines," answered the girl. 'I simply doubt I'd be able to do an adequate job for you."

"You will. My unfailing ability to spot the minutest speck of gold in the most mountainous pile of dross assures me," said Cardwell. "The moment I spied you in the Yellow Lion I knew I had discovered a brilliant new ornament for the world's stage."

"Good as gold," put in Bascom.

Digby smiled hopefully at her. "Will you join us, then? We'll see you're well looked after."

Alicia hesitated for a few seconds, then replied, "I will."

The footlights made a hazy border of brightness between her and the audience. The audience seemed to be a single immense dark shape, many-headed, lurking out there beyond the light and watching her intently.

Alicia stood stock still on the stage, one hand nervously twisting at a fold of the apron she wore as part of her costume. Here she was in the middle of the third act of *She Stoops to Conquer*, and all at once she couldn't remember what she was to say next.

Digby Grand, looking very sleek and dapper in the role of young Marlow, had just attempted to kiss her, mistaking Miss Hardcastle for a maid and her house for an inn.

The seconds, as each passed in turn, were of incredible length. Alicia feared the silence her forgetfulness was responsible for would drag on forever. And that the audience would soon grow restive and commence hooting and foot-stomping.

Digby, quickly sensing her problem, repeated his try at slipping an arm around her slim waist and pecking her on the cheek. "Pray, sir, keep your distance," he whispered in her ear.

She pulled away from him. "Pray, sir, keep your distance," she said, voice strong and containing only a slight quaver. "One would think you wanted to know one's age as they do horses, by mark of mouth."

"I protest, child, you use me extremely ill. If you keep me at this distance, how is it possible you and I can ever be acquainted?"

"And who wants to be acquainted with you? I want no such acquaintance, not I. . . ."

All the lines, the ones she'd pored over in her room by candlelight and rehearsed again and again with Digby as they journeyed by coach from one small town to another, returned to Alicia now. She began to speak Goldsmith's dialogue with ease. She became increasingly aware, could feel it, that the audience liked her and were responding to her. Never had she felt in her life before that particular elation which comes from making a gathering of people laugh and applaud.

When the act concluded, Alicia, slipping away from Cardwell who was portraying her quick-tempered father, moved off the small stage and located Digby.

"I think you saved me from being catcalled off the stage," she told him. "You make a most excellent prompter, Digby."

"Think nothin' of it," he said. "And as for the

groundlin's, why, lass, they dote on you. As do the folk in every blessed village we've honored with our company since you joined us last week."

Alicia smiled. "It's been so . . . well, entirely different from anything I've ever known," she said. "All in all . . . I'm enjoying myself a great deal. Except when I completely forget what I'm to say next."

"That's happened very little, Alicia," he said. "You're doing splendidly. I wager you're startin' to realize we're not near as dreadful as you anticipated. That some theater folk ain't the evil and rollickin' lot you've been led to believe."

"Rollicking, yes," said the girl, "but not at all evil. In fact, you've all become . . . my friends."

Grinning, Digby made a slight bow in her direction. "You, my dear, are fast becoming a very fine actress," he said. "I might go so far as . . . ah, but here comes the fourth act, and I must get ready for another of my brilliant entrances."

Alicia stayed in the darkness offstage and felt, for almost the first time since she'd fled from Rob and Lord MacQuarrie's estate, very nearly happy.

Chapter 27

Rob Kilgerrin said, "It's been a full week."

"A very long and fretful week, sir."

"I've scoured the blasted countryside, ridden from sunrise to dusk, questioned a multitude of people, and found not a trace of her."

"More's the pity, sir."

The young man was pacing the terrace of Lord MacQuarrie's country house. MacQuarrie himself had long since returned to London, but Kilgerrin was still here and using the place as a base from which to search for the missing Alicia.

"She left of her own free will, all evidence points to that."

"I quite agree, sir," said Rumsford, who was standing attentively by.

"We can only conclude she must have heard

Lord Mac and me arguing in the library that morning. He's a rather carrying voice."

"Like the boom of a cannon it is, sir."

"Yes, Alicia apparently overheard and, misunderstanding, ran away."

"Might I venture to suggest, as I have previously, sir, that it would have gone better had one confided in her much earlier in the game?"

"I wanted to, Rumsford. That's the very thing Lord Mac and I were quarreling about. He simply wouldn't allow me."

"There are times, sir, when one's heart must overrule one's sense of duty. So I believe, at any rate."

Kilgerrin paced in silence for a while. "The horse she took came home that very evening," he said at last. "By calculating how far it could travel to get someplace and back in that amount of time, I've a pretty fair idea of how far she rode before sending the horse away."

"Your mathematics and mapwork were both exemplary, sir."

"Then, by asking questions, I found people who'd actually seen her ride by," continued Kilgerrin, scowling. "It seemed indisputable, after piecing all the clues together, she'd gone somewhere in the vicinity of Middlesworth." He shook his head. "Yet hours of inquiring there yesterday produced nothing. It would have been market day when she arrived, very crowded and confused. Even so, you'd expect someone to have noticed a girl such as her. I can find no witness who remembers a lone auburn-haired girl. Indeed, many told me there were no strangers in Middlesworth that day save a nondescript troupe of wandering players."

"It seems unlikely, as you say, sir, that not a soul would take note of Miss Alicia."

Kilgerrin's scowl deepened. "Where is she?" He gazed at the surrounding trees and grass. "If she'd only given me a chance to explain myself before going from here that way."

"Perhaps, should one be fortunate, there'll be an opportunity to explain very soon."

"I'm going out to look for her again." Kilgerrin went striding away.

"Beastly cold."

"I consider a fire burning away in every fireplace to be a most unnecessary waste of fuel, doctor."

Marryat, hugging his spare frame, was staring into the great hollow fireplace in the sitting room of Lord Cranford's London townhouse. "Chills can lead to all sorts of complications," he complained.

"I never take sick, doctor," Lord Cranford informed him, running a finger along his beaklike nose. "Now then, what fresh news do you bring me?"

Dr. Marryat produced his snuffbox. "I made the dreadful journey down to Ravenshaw once again yesterday," he said. "Ah, what a state those fools are in. Copplestone, since his unsatisfactory audience here with you, has taken to imbibing large quantities of a very inferior port wine. He is in a state of continuing stupor while that old hag rants and raves and professes undying love for that annoying girl who—"

"Yes, yes, but do they know where she is?"

Marryat narrowed one eye, producing new wrinkles. "They no longer quite trust me, since they suspect I am more in sympathy with you than with them. Copplestone was obviously not soothed after his audience with you."

"I lied to the man, but perhaps he sensed that. There is no way around it, the girl must die—and soon."

"Even though they might wish to keep news from me," Marryat went on, "I feel I am able to get to the heart of things. It is my studied opinion that neither of them have any notion where Alicia Kingsley has gotten to."

"Time . . . there's little time."

"When do you think the invas—"

"You'll be told what you need to know when the time is ripe, doctor. Suffice it to say, we must destroy that girl very soon now." Cranford's knobby hand tightened on the back of the chair he stood behind. "We cannot afford to have the girl running around loose, she is like a lighted bomb that may explode at any moment and destroy us all."

"I wanted to kill her, right at the start."

A sneer touched Cranford's face. "Instead, however, you practiced your mumbojumbo on her, swearing to me the wench would never again remember what she'd witnessed," he said.

"The hypnotism was successful, may I remind you, for a good many months."

"But not for quite long enough, doctor."

"There is always the slender chance, when working with something as unpredictable as the human mind that—"

"Spare me any further excuses. I want that girl."

"You have men searching for her."

"Yes, and unable to locate her."

Dr. Marryat remembered to thrust a pinch of snuff into his nose. He inhaled, sneezed three times, sighed. "Kilgerrin may know something. The old woman told me he's been to Ravenshaw twice in search of the girl."

"That simple-minded dandy is being watched by one of my agents even as we speak, doctor. Thus far, Kilgerrin seems as much at a loss as we are."

"One young girl, alone and without a friend," mused Marryat. "Where on earth can she have gotten to?"

"I intend very soon to have an answer to that question," said Lord Cranford. "Alicia Kingsley must not remain alive very many days longer."

Chapter 28

Digby Grand offered his arm. "Will you allow me the pleasure of escortin' you on a tour of the quaint village of Molesworth?"

It was an overcast afternoon, and Alicia and the versatile young actor were standing in front of the George & Dragon Inn. The Cardwell Tragic & Comic Traveling Theater company had taken up residence there this morning, and Alicia was not due at the theater, more usually known as the grange hall, until after supper tonight.

"We seem to have quite a substantial crowd pouring into town," the girl remarked. "Surely not to attend our performance of *She Stoops to Conquer?*"

Digby's pliant face took on a conspiratorial cast, his head ticked closer to hers. "There's to be an exhibition of boxin' here today," he confided. "Goin' to occur on Priory Heath at the edge of this humble village. I think it might be most illuminatin' if we stroll through the streets of Molesworth and observe the bucks and swells flockin' here to indulge their interest in the Fancy. What say?"

Alicia shook her head negatively. She knew Rob Kilgerrin was an avid follower of boxing. It might well be he was coming to the village today. She could not risk being seen by him. "I don't mind crowds if the footlights separate me from them," she said. "But I don't relish mingling with them."

"No? To me this parade of dandies is like a pageant staged for my express amusement." Digby pointed, with a flourish, across the courtyard.

Through the arched entryway a portion of cobblestone street could be observed. Rolling along it now came an open barouche in which were perched four ample young men dressed most flamboyantly. Several small boys, barefoot and tattered, were trailing after the carriage, laughing and catcalling. Next came a coach and four, rattling impressively.

"Therein must ride a person of some rank in this world," commented Digby. "Note the filagree and that most impressive, though quite cryptic, coat of arms. Can those be sheep couchant?" Locking his hands behind his back, he sighed and leaned against the whitewashed wall of the inn. "Often I speculate, Alicia, about the possible turns my future may take. In my fancies I see myself being carried hither and yon in a gold-encrusted coach, with an abundance of lackies hangin' on to it and awaitin' my every command."

"That could well happen, you're an excellent actor, Digby."

He laughed. "Excellence is no guarantee of fortune," he told her. "In fact, the reverse is more often the case." Digby studied the girl's face for a few silent seconds. "It's my surmise you've known a much better style of life than that which is lived by wandering minstrels. Yet you never speak of your former life."

"I've no wish to."

"You've been a member of our carefree tribe near three weeks. Why, in that time the average young woman would have confided her entire tragic history as well as that of a good dozen of her friends and enemies."

Smiling faintly, the girl replied, "You must, then, forgive my uncommon habit of reticence."

"I don't pry, you know, so I may gossip to others," he told her. "If I am able to do anything, Alicia, it is to read character and feelings. My conclusions about you are that you are a most honest person, but that you are in some very troublesome situation. My services as knight errant or father confessor are at your—"

"Yes, I appreciate that." She put a hand on his arm. "At present, I've no need of either."

He made a resigned bow. "Since you won't go on the Grand Tour of Molesworth, I'll venture it alone," he said. "Might I, however, escort you to the theater this evening?"

"Yes, of course."

"Good. I shall anticipate that pleasant event throughout the remainder of this downcast day," Digby said. "I've a mind to attend the fisticuffs demonstration on the heath. I hear the bruisers are among the stars in the firmament of boxiana—one of them is the notorious Battlin' Bob Metz and the other glories in the nickname of the Brighton Butcher."

Alicia recognized the latter name. It was the man who'd greeted them on the night she and Rob Kilgerrin had visited the Vauxhall gardens. Yes, she'd have to remain close to the inn today and hope that after his bout the Butcher would be in no mood to attend a play.

"The fellow was absolutely fantastic," Digby was saying as they made their way along the twilight lane toward the grange hall. "Powerful, mind you, yet agile. He quite polished off Battlin' Bob in less than an hour."

Alicia nodded absently. "It seems I missed a great contest."

The streets of Molesworth were yet crowded. Many of those who'd traveled here to witness the boxing match had stayed on to celebrate at the inns and public houses of the village. Many very handsomely attired bucks were strolling the streets with newly acquired local belles on their arms.

"The Butcher assumed a stance much like this," Digby continued, detaching himself from the girl and demonstrating a pugilistic pose as they walked. "Then the fists flashed like bolts of lightning. Pam! Pam!" He punched at the air. "Battin' Bob was stunned, stupefied, groggy, out on his feet." Digby became Battlin' Bob, staggering and glassy-eyed. "It was a most marvelous contest."

"Yes, it certainly seems so," said Alicia, laughing. "The active, moving-about part of pugilism I believe I'd enjoy. Those fearful blows to the head and person are what would discourage me from seriously taking it up as a career."

"You already have quite a—"

"Lor, bless me!" A large thickset man with close-cropped hair had halted across the narrow street. He was in the company of a considerable group of friends, well-wishers, and awed females.

None of them understood the reason for his sudden halt.

But Alicia understood.

The thickset man was the Brighton Butcher, and he'd recognized her.

"Why, if it ain't Rob's young lady 'erself," exclaimed the fighter, starting across the street, with his puzzled entourage in tow. "Ain't this somethin', meetin' you this here way?"

"Do you know the fellow?" whispered Digby.

Paling, Alicia said, "No, he's mistaken me for someone else, obviously. Please, Digby, let's hurry to the theater."

Turning, Digby tipped his hat to the approaching pugilist. "Our compliments, sir, and may I add you're a most proficient and impressive gladiator," he called in a pleasant tone. "The lady fears, however, she knows you not. We find ourselves already late for our performance at the grange hall tonight of Goldsmith's immortal comedy, *She Stoops to Conquer*. Still a few choice seats remaining. With that, we bid you a most pleasant good evening." He took hold of Alicia's arm and started her walking away.

"Don't know me?" The Butcher stopped still on the cobblestones. "Blimey, I'd swear she's the very one me and Floss met up with at Vauxhall."

"Forget her," advised a yellow-haired young woman. "More likely she's snubbin' you."

The Butcher scratched at his lumpy skull. "Don't make no sense nohow."

He made no attempt to follow and allowed his followers to set him back on his original course.

When several hundred feet separated them from the group, Digby remarked, "You are indeed a woman of mystery."

"Yes, I fear so," she said, and smiled at him suddenly. "But when we become famous, think how useful that will be for keeping us in the London eye!"

Chapter 29

The man in gray called himself Dascoyne. He was lean, with a small pinched face, and gave the impression he never felt quite warm enough. He was sitting now, hunched, in the small cozy room which served the proprietor of the Yellow Lion Inn as an office. At the leaded windows a heavy afternoon rain was beating. "I'm not at liberty to say, sir," he was telling the somewhat uneasy innkeeper. "Let it be merely acknowledged that I serve certain persons very high in the government."

"I have no wish, far from it, to do anything that might offend the rulers of the land," said Mr. Bligh, for such was the name of the crinkly-haired man who operated the Yellow Lion. "Yet I can't for the life of me, and that's a fact, see exactly how—"

"We merely ask you, sir, to think, to remember," said Dascoyne, inching his chair nearer to that of the innkeeper. "A young girl is being sought. She is slender, aged two and twenty, with hair of a pale red hue. She is considered, by some, to be comely and is soft-spoken and demure."

Bligh shook his head. "Others have inquired after this very same young woman," he said. "She must, for a fact, be quite important. Would that I could—"

"We have good reason to believe she arrived in this very town on a recent market day, sir." Dascoyne unwound his thick gray wool muffler, bunched it between his hands. "Think harder, Mr. Bligh, strain, cudgel your brains. Surely the man who owns the most-frequented inn in Molesworth had a better opportunity of seeing this lone and friendless girl."

Bligh sat listening to the wind howling outside. He thought, strained, brow furrowed. "I wonder . . ."

Dascoyne leaned. "What is it you wonder, sir?"

"I do remember, and it only just this moment struck me, seeing a girl such as you described on the very day in question, yes," recalled Bligh. "Can't see how it can be the one you're all seeking, since this one wasn't alone, far from it."

"Even so, tell me what you can, provide me details, sir. Whom was she with?"

"Very striking young thing she was, very decent and upright she seemed, and yet she's apparently a notorious criminal of some sort being sought by sundry—"

"She's not a criminal, sir. Pray come to the point."

"I was about to remark it caused me to puzzle when I saw her with them—not their type, I'd have guessed. Though, if as you say, she's a famous murderess, well, then—"

"Whom was the girl with?" asked Dascoyne patiently.

"Why, Joshua Cardwell and his troupe," replied Bligh. "Perhaps you've heard of them in your travels. Cardwell's Tragic & Comic Theater?"

The gray man said, "I cannot recall having had the pleasure of witnessing their work upon the boards, sir. Am I correct in assuming this Cardwell tours the countryside hereabouts?"

"That he does. I'm told his *Macbeth* is quite an impressive show, full of witches and murders, although some judged it too violent for polite—"

"Yes, to be sure. This girl, you are certain, is now part of Cardwell's retinue?"

"Oh, yes, that she is. They dined here, right here in the Yellow Lion, on the very day you're all so curious about. Had two bottles of my best wine, giving a lie to the thought that actors are necessarily impoverished. Would that have been the day she committed this foul deed?"

"Would you know where Cardwell goes after he leaves this town, sir?"

"Almost always, for he visits us regular, twice a year, he goes from Middlesworth to Turbury, Woolsack, and then Molesworth. After that, I'm not at all clear as to his itinerary, having no real need to—"

"You've been a very great help, sir." Dascoyne stood up, rewound the thick muffler around his scrawny neck. "Perhaps your information will aid the cause I serve."

"Well, sir, that's comforting, to know I'm doing my bit. Before you journey on, may I offer you a small glass of—"

"No time, thank you all the same. I must pick up the trail of Cardwell without delay." He made a curt bow and hurried out into the hard rain.

Carriage wheels clanged on the cobblestones; horses' hooves splashed in the wide puddles of the street.

Rob Kilgerrin, deep in thought, paid the noise of the approaching vehicle little attention. Head down, he continued his walk along the rainswept London lane.

"Ahoy there, Rob, my boy!" bellowed someone from outside the carriage.

Kilgerrin spun and saw it drawing to a stop amid much splashing and rattling. "Thomas?"

Rowdybranch poked his cudgel out into the rain, beckoning. "I was en route to your townhouse in search of news of you when I spied you in the very flesh skulking along here like some freshly disinherited heir."

"I'm only in town for a day," explained the young man as he approached the carriage. "I came up to consult with Lord MacQuarrie. As you may know, Alicia continues to be—"

"Precisely why I am here. And the reason for my rousing myself from my snug eyrie to wander in this beastly London afternoon, my boy," the enormous artist informed him, flinging the door wide. "Climb aboard, will you, before you take on an even more woebegone and bedraggled aura."

"Have you learned something about her?" Eagerly, Kilgerrin entered and sat opposite his friend.

"Something you might have learned for yourself had you not been off in the woods and fens, sulking like Achilles in his tent."

"The girl I love is missing—she may well be dead, Thomas—and I've been driving myself half mad in searching for her. I don't find the situation a subject for levity."

"If the girl's already dead, my boy, my jests won't harm her, and if she still lives, which is very much the case, a quip or two is exactly what you need to cure you of this confounded state of self-pity you're in," the caricaturist told him as he settled back into his seat. "Plenty of time for sorrowful sentiments after we're each of us stretched out on our respective slabs and offering shelter to wayward worms."

"We see the world differently, Thomas." Kilgerrin got his temper under control. "What have you to tell me?"

"In the present instance I am but passing on knowledge," said Rowdybranch. "Yesterday your friend and mentor, the formidable gent known far and wide as the Brighton Butcher, paid me a visit in my humble studio above the print shop of the slow-witted Mrs. Draper. He was much perplexed, was the Butcher, and had taken the opportunity on returning to London after a stunning victory in the outlands to seek you out."

"I've been, as you possibly know, staying at Lord MacQuarrie's country estate."

"The Butcher was not aware of that," replied Rowdybranch. "Had I not been able to find some means of getting a message to you by way of your townhouse, I myself might well have had to undertake a pilgrimage out into the tree-infested wilderness in search of you."

"Come, what can the Brighton Butcher have to do with the whereabouts of Alicia?"

"He's seen her, my boy."

"What?" Kilgerrin gripped his friend's plump arm. "Where? When?"

"These are all pertinent and perceptive questions, Rob. Cease throttling my drawing arm and I'll proceed to answer them all in turn." He shifted his bulk and coughed. "After his pugilistic triumph in the backward and no doubt inbred village of Molesworth, the Butcher was strutting about the town and basking in the adulation of the simple-minded populace. Rustic bumpkins touched their forelocks to him, blushing nubile maidens cast inviting—"

"For the love of God, Thomas, spare me the colorful details and get to the nub of the business!"

"Friend Butcher saw Alicia, in the flesh and in the company of a young man. He greeted her and the girl was taken aback, but then pretended not to know him," explained Rowdybranch. "Being a fellow more noted for his physical than his mental prowess, the Butcher allowed himself to be persuaded he'd made a mistaken identification. As he brooded over the incident in the ensuing days, however, he convinced himself he had been right and decided to ask you exactly what was what. Not locating you at home and having no idea where to seek you, he hied himself to my humble studio, knowing that you and I are as close as such other sets of chums as Damon and Pythias, Roland and—"

"What the devil was Alicia doing in Molesworth with this young man?"

"The lad was an actor. He gave the Butcher the impression he and the young lady were part of a traveling play company."

"Actors?" Kilgerrin frowned for a few seconds, then laughed. "Well, still and all, this is splendid news, Thomas. We now know where she was but a few days ago. All I need do is find out the name and itinerary of this touring—"

"Spare yourself the effort, my boy. This particular group calls itself the Cardwell Comic & Tragic somethingorother," Rowdybranch informed his young friend. "Before embarking on my breathless quest for your person, I asked a few pithy questions of my theatrical friends in Drury Lane and Covent Garden. I have ascertained that Joshua Cardwell's was the only company of roving thespians to appear in Molesworth in recent times and that after their performances there they journeyed next to Market Soglough, Mudbury, and thence to Stunbridge, whereat they are appearing this very day, and the morrow as well."

"Then that's where I must go," said Kilgerrin, reaching for the door handle.

"One moment, Rob," said Rowdybranch. "I know some of what transpired, and of the forces in motion here. Be certain you are open and forthright with the girl henceforward. And be on your guard lest both of you be killed."

Chapter 30

All at once she fainted.

She felt a sudden pain deep inside her, as though she'd been struck by a clenched fist. Consciousness seemed to drain out of her and, swaying to the left and then the right, Alicia toppled down on the rough wood floor of the meeting hall.

She was aware of Digby's crying out and of Joshua running toward her. The sound of their feet on the boards faded, grayness surrounded her, then blackness and, swiftly, nothingness.

The rehearsal had started well, and she'd anticipated nothing unusual. The acting company had arrived in Stunbridge late on a blustery, rain-sodden afternoon and, after partaking of a rather lavish tea at the Black Swan Inn, where they would be staying, Cardwell had brought his company to the nearby meeting hall, which would serve as their theater during their two days in the village. The play was a new one which Alicia was not familiar with—a tragedy entitled *The Fratricide,* in which she was to play the much put-upon young daughter of the Duke of Macri.

Digby, whose job it was to look after such things, provided her with a neatly transcribed copy of her part in the first act. "A very movin' work this is," he explained, as he seated himself beside her on a roughhewn bench. "Much blood-lettin' and screamin', in the best Italian style. Old Walpole himself would be proud of *The Fratricide.* Deals with a wicked uncle who murders, by means of a fiendishly clever poison, his own brother. His niece chances to witness, unbeknownst to him . . . why, what's ailin' you, my girl?"

Alicia had pressed her hand to her breast, her face going pale. She shook her head slowly from side to side, puzzled. "I . . . don't really know . . . nothing is wrong, Digby," she managed to say. "It was only that I felt . . . well, very giddy all at once."

"Forgive this liberty," Digby said as he took hold of her chill hand and started rubbing it. "Can it be you've taken a chill? This life upon the road can play havoc with you until you become accustomed to it. Why, when the late Mrs. Snell was travelin' with us two seasons ago, she was forever sneezin' and coughin'. Not that life upon the stage was, I hasten to add, what finally took her off. No, 'twas a carter's wagon which ran her down in White Chapel whilst she was in the midst of celebratin', with the aid of several tankards of stout and two husky midshipmen, her, or leastwise so she claimed, twenty-eighth birthday. Possibly the strain of celebratin' the ruddy birthday so many times over the years had—"

"I'm quite all right now," assured Alicia, managing a smile. "We can, I think, proceed." Taking the sheets of script from him, she began turning them.

"You make your entrance, and a rather fiery and impassioned one it is, in scene two of Act One. You're clad in your nightdress, hair in disarray and blood besmearin' you quite liberally. Said blood, by the way, comes not from your father, who is still alive and kickin' at this point in the tragic events, but from the gory corpse of Prince Prigio. 'What fateful portents do I read in this blood-bedewed corpse,' you wail, eyes wide with horror. 'Prince Prigo, the playmate of my, alas, gone childhood, lies dead, cold and gruesome beyond yon arras. Aye, methinks 'twill next be my own much-loved father who I'll find wallowing in his own gore, throat cut and a bloody grin quite superimposed upon his dear—' I say, are you certain you're still not feelin' a bit peckish?"

Uncalled-for images were crowding into her mind. She saw her father lying dead. Not in bed, as she'd thought she remembered him, but sprawled in the dirt. A look of terrible anguish etched deep on his waxy face, blood spurting out of a black hole in his chest and spilling, gushing, across the front of his waistcoat. She was standing near him, gazing down in horror. A pistol. There was a pistol in the hand of . . .

She realized she was standing on her feet.

Digby was saying something to her. ". . . bit of fresh air?"

"I'm very sorry . . . something in this play . . . reminds me of . . ."

She fainted.

166

Her father spoke to her. "It's all there," he was telling her. "It's all there," he was telling her in his familiar voice. "The truth is at Ravenshaw, pet, to be found out."

"I'll die if I return."

"No, you must go back."

She couldn't keep looking at him, at his face of a bluish color, his gleaming eyes thick-rimmed with sooty black. His teeth seemed too large; the flesh of his lips had already begun to rot away.

"I can't!"

"Yes! Promise you'll return and find the truth." He began perspiring, and each drop which appeared on his face was the color of fresh blood. "Promise!"

"Yes, all right, I promise, Father. But please . . ."

She was talking not to her dead father, but to Valerie. Sitting up in bed, clutching the older woman's hand, Alicia came slowly back to herself.

"Be easy, dear," the actress said in comforting tones.

"I . . . was I babbling?"

"A bad dream, I imagine you were merely having a bad dream," Valerie soothed. "Lie back, try to get some—"

"I'm not ill, Valerie, truly I'm not."

"I'd say you may well be coming down with something, dear. This pattern of life is new to you, the stress of it at first can wear you down."

"It was only a temporary spell." They'd apparently carried her to her room at the inn, placed her on her bed fully clothed. Taking hold of the carved bedpost nearest her, Alicia pulled herself off the bed. She felt a bit unsteady, but was able to mask the feeling. Twilight was already showing at the small round windows. "I'll be able to go on tonight."

"Not at all," said Valerie, "you will rest until tomorrow. Digby is already selecting his wigs so he can do your part as—"

"Really, Valerie, I mustn't let you all down this way," said the girl. "You must return to the theater and inform them I'm feeling absolutely fine. I intend to rehearse with you and go on this very night."

The raven-haired actress hesitated. "Are you certain you're up to it?"

"Of course."

"Very well. Should you feel at all poorly, summon me and I'll come rushing back."

"No need to fear, I'll be with you all shortly."

After the actress had left, Alicia hurried to the place behind the heavy bureau where she'd hidden the pouch containing her store of ready cash. With that in hand, she gathered the few belongings she'd acquired since joining the company and packed them into her new portmanteau.

Alicia knew what she must do next. She had to return to Ravenshaw. The truth was there.

Chapter 31

A light rain had begun to fall. Cloak wrapped tightly around her, Alicia stood under the slanting roof of the livery stable and talked to the rake-thin old man who ran the place. "I'll pay whatever you wish," she persisted.

"Ain't a question of money, missy," he said, clamping his few teeth down on the stem of his unlit pipe. "Issue at hand is, I got not a carriage to rent to ye this night. An' if I did, which I ain't, I'd still have no one to drive 'em. For Evan Heyman is down with a most awful case of the grippe an' Billy Anmar's up to no good with the Widow Midges an' the good Lord only knows when, or even if, the lad'll e'er return. Romance can ruin a man."

"Very well," said the anxious girl, "let me hire a horse, then."

The old man's wispy white eyebrows rose. "Are you aft to tellin' me as how you'd ride alone across this devilish countryside all the way to this here Ravenshaw Court, a good thirty miles if it's an inch? Why, what if brigands set upon you an' ravished you? What'd become of me horse then?"

"The roads hereround are relatively safe," Alicia told him. "I'll pay a fair sum for the use of him. And leave the animal at Jud Hurd's stable in Danbury, which is very near Ravenshaw Court. You have but to send a boy to—"

"Oh, I know Jud, an' a fairer man ne'er lived, but I doubt you'll ever reach him. No, no, missy, the risk is much too fearful."

Alicia sighed out her exasperation. She had successfully slipped away from the inn, and she had to get to Ravenshaw as soon as possible. "Listen, then, suppose I buy one of your horses outright. Then if we're both slaughtered by wild beasts or highwaymen, it will be no concern of yours."

The old man scratched his head. "Sell you one of me horses, is it? Well now, missy, these creatures are like family to me, better than family, since they be much more dependable and a good deal pleasanter to gaze upon than any of my kin. Oh, to persuade me to part with even the least of them would cost a—"

"How much?"

Before the old stablekeeper could reply, a lean figure stepped in out of the shadows at the entrance of the stable and into the circle of light cast by an overhead lantern. "Forgive my intruding into what is quite obviously a private business discussion," he said politely. He was dressed in clerical garb, and there was a beatific smile on his lean face. "I am the Reverend Dascoyne, and I fear I overheard some of your conversation, miss."

Alicia studied the man. He seemed a prim and rather fussy man of the cloth. "I am anxious to get to Ravenshaw Court near Danbury."

"Truly, as I've long believed, the Lord oft takes a hand in even the most petty affairs of man," said the man who called himself Dascoyne. "I am myself bound for Danbury to visit a dear cousin who, so a hastily dispatched letter informs me, may be at death's door. I pray I may reach his bedside in time to help him prepare himself for that great journey which each of us must someday make." He glided closer to the girl. "The Lord's will it must have been which prompted me to stop, after a long and weary day of travel, at the Black Swan for a hasty supper before continuing on. Might I offer you a ride in my own carriage, miss? It lies within this very stable at the moment."

"Thought you told me you was—"

"Never mind, my good man," Dascoyne hastily said to the old stablekeeper. "I'll settle with you at once, if you don't mind."

"Don't mind a bit." He held out a hand and named a sum which covered the care of the horses and a few other incidentals.

The spurious priest payed him, taking the money purse out of a coat pocket which also contained a small prayer book. "If you are ready, miss, we can very shortly depart."

Alicia picked up her portmanteau. "This is truly most kind of you."

"I fear I'll be dull company for a vivacious young

lady such as yourself," he said with a modest smile. "Most of my time on the road I like to devote to prayer and contemplation."

"I won't mind," the girl said. "I have much to contemplate myself."

The rain kept increasing as their carriage rattled through the dark night. It was pounding on the roof now, splashing on the muddy road.

Dascoyne sat with eyes nearly shut, prayer book clasped in knobby hands.

They'd been traveling nearly an hour, and Alicia was commencing to be concerned. She leaned forward once again, peering out of the window into the rain. "Are you certain your driver knows what he's about, Reverend Dascoyne?"

His eyes clicked open. "Beg pardon?"

"I'm almost certain we've taken a wrong turning. This road will not bring us anywhere near Danbury."

Smiling blandly, Dascoyne said, "Oh, we're not going to Danbury, Miss Kingsley."

She pushed back against her seat, staring at him. "What do you mean?"

"I mean, quite simply, that you are being taken to an out-of-the-way cottage where you'll be questioned by certain people," he explained. "After which you'll be, as painlessly as possible, done away with and buried in the woods."

"You're with them! With Lord Cranford and the others!"

"One of his most loyal agents, yes," admitted Dascoyne. "I've been on your trail for many a day, young lady, and it's glad I am I adapted the guise of a pious clergyman for this phase of my quest. It allowed me to gull you quite nicely. I detest a violent and messy abduction."

"You won't keep me here," she said, lunging for the door.

Very calmly Dascoyne grabbed her arm and pulled her to him before she could open the carriage door. He was surprisingly strong, and he twisted her arm up behind her with ease. "I'm quite adept at this sort of thing, my dear, and no amount of struggling will avail you. We're almost to our destination. If you try any further to escape I, I assure you, shall break your arm. At the very least."

Chapter 32

"Ain't she the pretty one, now," observed the one-eyed man. "Seems a ruddy shame to do 'er in. "Mightn't I 'ave 'er when we're through?" He was large, his face stubbled with gray and black whiskers. He wore the simple clothes of a woodsman, and the smell of him and the splotches of blood upon his ragged coat testified to the fact that part of his living was made as a poacher. "I'd be most nice to 'er, I would. You'd like 'at, wouldn't you, miss?" He touched her face with coarse fingers, pinched her cheek, then took hold of her chin between thumb and forefinger and tilted her head up.

"I'd rather be killed," Alicia said.

The small man in the corner laughed. "Most wenches feels that way 'bout Ludd."

"Gentlemen," said Dascoyne evenly, "that will be quite enough."

Grumbling, Ludd sat back down in his wood and leather chair. "Jist tryin' to pass the bloody time."

Dascoyne had brought her to a ramshackle stone cottage on the edge of an unfamiliar woodland. With the help of Ludd and the small man he'd tied her to a chair beside a lopsided wooden table. There was a small fireplace, with a turf fire fuming slowly in it. The rain slapped down on the thatched roof.

"If I can't 'ave 'er for me own," said Ludd, rubbing at his gaping eye socket, "kin I at least be the one what gits to do 'er in?"

"That will be decided when the others arrive," said Dascoyne.

"He'll fool with her first," prophesied the little man huddled on the floor in the corner of the cottage. "That's exactly what he'll do. Best let me use me knife, sir."

" 'At ain't neat," said Ludd. "I'll promise you I kin do it quick an' easy, with nary a drop of blood or nothin'. Snap 'er pretty neck is what I'll do, see. I been doin' it to deer of late, an' it works most effective, it does. Won't hardly hurt, miss."

Alicia ignored him and turned to Dascoyne. "Eventually, you know, someone will catch up with you. You'll be hanged for this."

"Within a very few weeks at most, Miss Kingsley, this country will no longer be ruled by a madman and a fat libertine, but rather by a man of infinite genius. From that moment on, those of us who possess real merit will cease to be ignored and cast aside. We will take our rightful places in the governing of this country, rule those who up to now have turned their pompous backs on us."

"He's going to be a blooming prince once Nappy comes over to sit on the throne," said the little man in the corner. "Wear a crown, don't you know, and have little goldy-haired lads carryin' his train around."

Dascoyne scowled at him. "My position won't be quite so lofty, Bagot."

"I think not," mumbled Bagot.

The one-eyed man was staring at Alicia again. "You're 'bout near the prettiest thing what I've ever seen," he announced. "Goin' to bust me 'eart 'avin' to throttle you and dump your pretty carcass in a dirty old pit with lime an' all in it an'—"

"Enough of that, Ludd," warned Dascoyne.

Alicia said, "You can't seriously believe Napoleon can successfully invade our country?"

"Ah, but quite obviously I do."

"Any such attempt must fail miserably. Only a fool would pin his hopes on such a fantastic dream."

"Then you must put me down for a fool, my dear, since—"

"What's 'at?" Ludd shot to his feet, glaring at the door.

Dascoyne said, "I heard nothing."

"Outside."

"It's just Mildmay," said Bagot. "He's probably restless, having to look after the bloody horses."

"I got mos' keen ears." Ludd eased over to the wooden door and stood listening. "Somethin's wrong, I swear." From inside his splattered jacket he drew a pistol. "Goin' to have me a look."

"Very well, if it will calm you down," said Dascoyne with a patronizing smile.

Ludd inched the door open and stood on the threshold gazing out into the rainy darkness. After a few seconds he slipped outside and shut the door, silently, behind him.

"He's awful good with rabbits," observed the little man in the corner. "I mean, he can hear 'em a good half-mile off. Never much cared for the taste of rabbit meself, but if you do, Ludd's sure the bloke to catch plenty of the things."

The rain kept hitting the thatched roof; the fire sputtered. Minutes dragged by. Ludd did not return.

Dascoyne said finally, "What in the devil is he up to out there?"

"He's very thorough, is Ludd."

Another minute passed, two more. The one-eyed man remained absent.

Dascoyne rose up from his chair, bones crackling. "Bagot, you had better find out what's keeping that idiot."

"Aw, he'll be back soon enough."

"Outside, now."

With a complaining groan, the little man unfolded himself to his full height and went shuffling across the floor. A knife appeared in his left hand. "If there's aught the matter, sir, I'll settle it." He moved out into the night.

"Perhaps," suggested Alicia as the door closed, "you're surrounded by those who've come in search of me."

Dascoyne chuckled. "Who might they be? Surely not that raggle-taggle crew of threadbare actors? It takes all the courage they can muster simply to face an audience," he said with a smirk. "Or can it be you suppose Rob Kilgerrin has gathered an army of his fellow fops and come hunting for you?"

Alicia lowered her head, not answering.

"No, my dear," continued the self-satisfied Dascoyne, "you are quite alone in this wicked world, and none care a farthing for—"

The dusty window just above his head all at once came smashing in, showering him with jagged shards of rain-beaded glass.

Dascoyne sprang around to face the window, hand darting toward the pistol in his waistband.

"Not at all a wise thing to do," advised Rob Kilgerrin, who stood at the window opening with a cocked pistol pointing in directly at the lean man. "Instead, my friend, extract that weapon of yours, most cautiously, and drop it to the floor where I can see it. Thereafter, hasten to untie the young lady. Any hesitations or attempts at trickery, and your meager flesh will stop a pistol ball."

Dascoyne took the gun out, swallowing hard, and let it fall to the planks of the floor. "So Miss Kingsley has a champion after all," he said.

Chapter 33

"A very neat job," said Kilgerrin, stepping back to admire the job he'd done of trussing up Dascoyne. "You look ready to be delivered by Father Christmas."

"Futile," said Dascoyne. "In a matter of weeks the forces of Napoleon shall—"

"That's extremely doubtful. Since by tomorrow all England will know of Lord Cranford's treachery," Kilgerrin told him. "All your grand plans will collapse, my friend, and go blowing away on the wind."

The other two men and the carriage driver had already been tied up and left outside in the night rain. During the wrapping up of Dascoyne, Alicia spoke only a few words to Rob. She'd, on his instructions, picked up Dascoyne's discarded pistol and held it aimed at the man until Rob had entered the cottage and set to work.

"I picked up your trail in Danbury," Kilgerrin had explained. "Arrived there too late to keep this imitation cleric from abducting you, but soon enough to learn from your stableman which direction your carriage had taken."

"Yes, I see."

"I was able to track your carriage to this god-forsaken hut," Kilgerrin had continued. "Dispatching the driver who waited outside was no great challenge and then, while I still reconnoitered, that great loutish Cyclops came blundering out. I was able to lay him out beside his associate, and then the third one made his appearance."

"Yes, I see," she repeated dully.

Now Dascoyne was safely incapacitated, and there was no more to do in the cottage. "Come," said Kilgerrin, taking the girl by the arm, "I'll see you return safely to London."

Alicia allowed him to escort her out into the rain and dark without speaking. Once clear of the cottage, she pulled free of him. "I don't intend to go back to London as yet."

"Don't tell me the life of a wandering player is so appealing you intend—"

"I must go to Ravenshaw."

He stared at her, the rain hitting at his handsome face. "That's not safe, Alicia. Lord, I can't allow you to do—"

"Have you been instructed by your masters to prevent me from returning to my own home? Do they have other plans for me?"

"So you did hear what Lord Mac and I were saying on that morning," he said.

"Oh, yes, I heard that you didn't love me at all, that you'd merely been hired to spy on my family and I was considered the weakest link." Her nostrils were flaring, her breasts rising and falling rapidly. "Rob, I believed so much in you, I thought you were the only man in the whole round world I could trust. I actually believed you loved me."

"I do love you." He took her by the shoulders. "Listen to me, Alicia. I know full well I should have told you long ago I worked as a government agent, that my job is to ferret out spies and traitors and those who believe in Bonaparte and his insane plans to conquer England. I didn't, though, and I regret it greatly. I kept things from you, I admit. Yet, you must believe this, I never lied to you. When I said I loved you, Alicia, it was true. True."

The rain was hitting down hard on both of them. The girl slowly shook her head. "I'll never believe you again." She twisted out of his grasp. "Now, please, I must—"

"Why? Why do you insist on returning to that place?"

"Because I've been remembering," she answered. "Something terrible happened at Ravenshaw Court, involving my father and me and my Uncle Toby. I feel certain if I return, if I see again all the familiar places, I'll remember everything and know the truth at last."

Kilgerrin said, "Very well, I'll accompany you."

"No, I don't want that," she told him. "In these past few weeks, Rob, I've learned some valuable lessons. I've learned I can fend for myself, can earn a modest living if need be, and don't have to depend on any—"

"Yes, and you should also have learned that there

are unscrupulous men who'd kill you, given half a chance," Kilgerrin cut in. "Some of those men lie bound hereabouts, Alicia, but others still roam at large. You are far from safe."

"I'd rather risk danger than have to relie on you to—"

"Alicia, I must stay with you." He caught her up in his strong arms, pulled her close to him, and, in spite of her initial protest, kissed her, long and hard. "I do love you."

The girl said nothing for several seconds. Tears were running down her cheeks, but the rain washed them swiftly from her cheeks. "I . . . I want to believe in you . . . yet . . ."

"We'll make use of this fellow's carriage which stands here idle, and I'll return for my own mount later." He swept her up in his arms and lifted her into the carriage which had conveyed her here. "Settle yourself in there, and I'll drive this thing. With any luck, we'll reach Ravenshaw Court in little more than two hours."

She smiled hopefully and settled back into her seat.

Chapter 34

The rain had stopped, and the black was very slowly starting to drain out of the sky as dawn approached. On foot, hand in hand, Alicia and Rob were moving toward the stable area of the Ravenshaw estate. They'd left the carriage partially hidden in a stand of dark elms.

The girl felt both excitement and dread. Some part of her mind warned her away from here, urged her to flee. Alicia ignored that and persisted.

"What is it we're to find here?" Kilgerrin asked.

Alicia replied, "The truth . . . that's all I'm really certain of."

Birds were awakening in the woodlands around Ravenshaw Court, announcing the fact with enthusiastic chirping and song. The horizon beyond the large house was shining with a thin blue.

The girl pulled Kilgerrin suddenly into a pass-way between two of the whitewashed stable build-ings. A horse stomped and snorted uneasily within one of the stalls. "We want to go . . . around this way."

She moved slowly now and mechanically, al-most like a somnambulist. Yet her eyes were open wide and she was frowning, looking very carefully all around her.

They were at the rear of one of the low shingle-roofed buildings, almost hidden from the main house by trees and shrubs.

Alicia stopped, felt the breath going out of her.

Rob's hand tightened on hers. "What's wrong?"

"Here, this is right," she said in a murmuring voice. She got her respiration under control and pointed into the wooded area. "There's a tiny little path in there, Rob, a shortcut I made myself over the years by coming down here to peek at my favor-ites and slip them treats pilfered from the kitchen."

Kilgerrin remained silent, watching her pale face.

"That night," she said slowly. "The night my fa-ther died . . . yes, I can see it all . . . I was restless. Perhaps I sensed something was going on wrong. I threw a cloak over my shoulders and came out for a walk . . . the hour was near midnight." She paused and ran her tongue over her dry lips. "Rob, they tried to make me forget . . . but it's all flooding back. . . ."

"Go carefully, dear. Don't upset yourself."

"As I . . . approached the stables—they didn't know I was anywhere near—I heard them arguing . . . violently. It was my father and . . . that dreadful little doctor . . . and my Uncle Toby." Her eyes were nearly shut, she was seeing into the past, seeing it clearly for the first time in many long months. "Fa-ther was saying, 'You're a traitor, my own brother-in-law! These documents prove it, the papers you tried to hide from me, Tobias.'" The girl held her hand as though she had a sheaf of papers in it, rattling them. "He told Uncle Toby, 'All this time you've been living under my roof, you've been using these grounds as a place to meet with these treacherous scoundrels who would give our country over to the likes of Bonaparte.' My uncle was frightened, shaking. 'I believe in this cause with all my heart,' he insisted to my father. 'I know Bonaparte will soon rule us, and when he does, then I'll no longer be simply your impoverished brother-in-law living off your dole. No, I'll be—' 'You'll be in the Tower or on the gallows,' my father told him. 'For I intend to inform the authorities about you and this rascal, Marryat, and all the rest of your miserable crew, Tobias.' That was when Marryat spoke. 'We have to stop him, Tobias! Now, swiftly!' And then Uncle Toby . . . he drew out his pistol and pointed it at my father. I . . . I'd been standing, nearly frozen with fear, in the woods yonder, only a few hundred feet away. Now I started to run toward them, to cry out. 'Don't, Uncle Toby! No, don't!' Even as I ran I heard the pistol shots. There . . . I still cannot remember exactly those next few seconds . . . I was kneeling beside my father, and the life was spilling out of him and there was blood all over the front of him . . . and I had blood all over my hands . . . Uncle Toby was sobbing, the terrible pistol shaking in his hand . . . and Dr. Marryat was watching it all with those awful, burning eyes . . . and . . . then I must have fainted."

Kilgerrin put an arm around her shoulders. "That's enough, Alicia. No need to—"

"Don't stop me now. This thing . . . it's been festering within me for so many long months . . . I must get it all out . . . for good and all. I remember next awakening in my own room and . . . they were circled round my bed . . . Dr. Marryat and Uncle Toby and Aunt Elizabeth . . . watching me as they bickered amongst themselves. 'Kill her,' the little doctor urging. Aunt Liz wouldn't stand for that . . . they argued and argued . . . and finally they agreed I was to live and Dr. Marryat was to . . . to hypnotize me, put me into some sort of trance and make me forget forever everything I'd seen that night."

"Yes, I've long suspected that."

"It was . . . terrible. He forced me to drink some bitter potion . . . they held me, the others, and he forced it down my throat. I . . . everything went spinning, and the three of them changed shapes . . . and then it was only his eyes, burning into mine . . . probing into my brain like a glowing poker. He told me . . . told me over and over . . . my father had suffered a fit and died . . . I had seen nothing, heard nothing, down by the stables . . . when I awakened I would believe firmly my poor father had died from purely natural causes. As soon as all the funeral obligations were out of the way . . . I would go to London and live with Queen Bess in our townhouse. I would find I didn't much care for Ravenshaw Court any more. Hated it, in fact, and wouldn't want to visit here very often at all."

"So they could use this place as a base for their own operations."

The girl nodded, sighed, rested her head against his broad chest. "Why did they do all this to me? Why didn't they simply kill me?"

"Because we loved you," said her Uncle Tobias. He was standing a few yards from them with a pistol in his hand.

Chapter 35

"Loved me?"

Tobias Copplestone was fully dressed, although his clothes were in some disarray. His face was puffy; there were traces of earlier meals on both his cheeks and his wrinkled cravat. The hand holding the pistol was a bit unsteady. "Often come down here of a morning," he said. "First couldn't stand being anywhere near. Of late felt drawn. Perhaps the spirit of your late father . . . will let me tell him how very sorry—"

"Might I suggest," cut in Kilgerrin, "you put that pistol away, sir. There's been quite enough violence done to Alicia already."

"Really believe must do away with you. Both of you," said the older man. "Can't have you betraying us. Not when Bonaparte is so near making a move. So much time and effort—"

"Listen to me, Uncle Toby." Alicia pulled away from Rob and walked toward her uncle.

Rob said, "Alicia, careful with—"

"You aren't going to kill me!" she told her uncle, facing him, anger strong on her face, hands defiantly on her narrow hips. "Hand me that pistol. Let's have no more of this."

Copplestone took a step back. "Didn't want to kill you before, dear," he said in an unsteady voice. "Marryat did. Elizabeth quite stubborn about it. So was I, believe me. Can't kill such a lovely young thing. Not even for Napoleon Bonaparte himself. Mesmerize the child instead. Safer. Yes. Worked splendidly. Then you spoiled it, began to remember. Have to do it again. Cranford, brilliant man, make a great leader after the invasion. No heart. Took it out of my hands, do you see. Went to him, pleaded. He lied. Assured me you wouldn't be harmed. Give Marryat another chance. Lied. All the while plotting. Brilliant man. No heart. Now? Must do it myself, I fear. You know everything. Date of important events too close."

"I don't believe you can kill me," the girl told him. "You wouldn't have killed my father if Marryat hadn't goaded you into it." She moved even nearer and held out her hand.

Copplestone retreated another step. "Got to, don't you see? Invasion almost upon us. You and this lad talk. Very bad. Walls come tumbling down. House of cards. Bad. No heart. All go to the gibbet. Even dear Elizabeth. All for naught. End of family. Don't want to. What else is there?"

The girl stretched out her hand until it was nearly touching the barrel of the gun. "You killed my

188

father, but you can't kill me. Please now, give me the pistol."

"Killed own kin. Almost a brother to me. Bible. Cain and that other chap. Horror." He took two steps back, a new light in his eyes. "Another answer." The pistol swung up to his temple, and his finger squeezed the trigger.

"Alicia!" Rob's voice shouted above the sound of the shot. He ran, caught the girl's arm, pulled her away.

Copplestone had gone staggering to the right. He fell to his knees, stumbled, swayed. His body jerked three times, and he fell to one knee. Death took him over then and slammed him over into the dawn-wet grass.

Kilgerrin said, "Perhaps this is best," he said, looking down at the old man. "Come away from here before you—"

"It's all right, Rob," she said in a low voice. "I think I'm beyond fainting . . . and beyond shedding any more tears. For a time, anyway."

Chapter 36

The house in Darkside Square was different. There seemed to be more sunlight in its rooms, and the rooms were decorated with pleasant papers and paints; the furnishings all radiated comfort and warmth.

Alicia, in a high-bodiced gown, was sitting on a loveseat with a cup of tea in her hand. "Yes, I suppose I might," she was saying to Rob Kilgerrin. "My period of mourning can be considered over, I do think. A bit soon, but another little touch of scandal won't matter."

"Thomas promises it will be a most splendid dinner party," said Kilgerrin from his position near the bow-window. "The guests will be, by standards of London society, somewhat unusual. We may expect Joshua Cardwell, Miss Valerie, and Digby Grand.

I'll be there, of course, as well as the Brighton Butcher and his Floss. Rowdybranch is also allowing Mrs. Draper a place at the festive table, since she's turning over her spacious dining room to him for the evening."

"It sounds like a very exceptional gathering," the girl said. "I'll be delighted to see my friends again after these past few weeks of near isolation."

Kilgerrin cleared his throat. "Lord MacQuarrie has also indicated he'll attend the fete, unless that would unsettle you, Alicia."

She shook her head. "Not at all. He is, after all, the man you work for."

"He'd like, I'm certain, to make amends for some of the past misunderstandings which have existed," said Rob. "He's also, I might add, in a much more cordial mood of late. Due in good part to the fact that we've been able to round up, due in part to the information your Aunt Elizabeth provided, Lord Cranford's entire organization."

"Aunt Elizabeth," said Alicia. "I wonder if she'll be happy in Australia."

"There's a great opportunity for a woman of her sort there, and she does have a few friends who've resettled near Sydney."

The girl nodded. "Since she's also taking Dante with her, I am encouraged. Those two should be able to subdue the most untamed of wildernesses."

Kilgerrin closed the room and seated himself next to her. "And you do understand and agree I must continue to work as I have?"

"Perfectly. We've, I do believe, quite adequately thrashed all this out, Rob. There is one further thing, however...."

"Yes?"

"It occurs to me that Thomas Rowdybranch's forthcoming dinner party might be exactly the right place to announce our impending marriage."

The young man blinked, then grinned. "Then you've accepted my proposal?"

"Oh, yes. Had I neglected to tell you?"

"I've been in some doubt, yes."

"Forgive me, perhaps I've been teasing you because of the way you once kept the truth from me," Alicia said. "I must put aside such feelings from now on. Yes, Rob, I very much wish to be your wife, and there's never really been any doubt in my mind."

Outside a fine carriage rolled solemnly by, the DeLacy boy came sneaking from his home to have another try at bird-killing in the square's little park, and old Mr. Ferris was busy scouring his front steps into a spotless state. In other words, the world was going on just exactly as it always had. Unaware of the momentous events taking place within Alicia's drawing room.